DOVE

DOVE

Barbara Hanrahan

University of Queensland Press
St Lucia·London·New York

By the same author

The Scent of Eucalyptus
Sea-Green
The Albatross Muff
Where the Queens all Strayed
The Peach Groves
The Frangipani Gardens

Published by University of Queensland Press, St Lucia, Queensland, 1982

Second printing 1983

Typeset by Hedges & Bell, Maryborough, Victoria.
Second printing by The Dominion Press—Hedges & Bell, Maryborough 3465

Distributed in the United Kingdom, Europe, the Middle East, Africa, and the Caribbean by Prentice-Hall International, International Book Distributors Ltd., 66 Wood Lane End, Hemel Hempstead, Herts., England.

Published with the assistance of the Literature Board of the Australia Council.

The quotation on the dedication and epigraph page is from William Faulkner's *Requiem for a Nun* (London: Chatto and Windus Ltd, 1953).

National Library of Australia
Cataloguing-in-Publication data

Hanrahan, Barbara, 1939-.
  Dove.

  ISBN 0 7022 1880 4.
  ISBN 0 7022 1890 1 (pbk.).

  I. Title. (Series: Paperback prose).

A823′.8

Library of Congress
Cataloguing-in-Publication data

Hanrahan, Barbara.
  Dove.

  (Paperback prose, ISSN 0156 6628)
  I. Title.
PR9619.3.H3D6   823   81-19652
ISBN 0-7022-1880-4   AACR2
ISBN 0-7022-1890-1 (pbk.)

To my father,
WILLIAM MAURICE HANRAHAN
(Bob)
1914–1940

The past is never dead. It's not even past.
William Faulkner

The author gratefully acknowledges the assistance of the
Literature Board of the Australia Council

Prologue
Arden Valley

The giantess was buried in the cemetery by the Lutheran church. It was the expressed wish of the deceased that her remains should be conveyed to their last resting place in the spring cart in which she used to travel about the country when on tour. A hearse led the funeral and was filled with wreaths. The spring cart with the remains followed. It took six men, including a brother of the deceased, to carry the coffin to the grave; eight men with a double set of four ropes were required to lower it.

She'd been Miss Scholz, the German Giantess, who weighed thirty stone. Crystal read it on the banner, which had done duty as an advertising sign — which now draped the coffin.

It was perfect. Yellow letters on crimson silk; so much funereal black, tightly buttoned. Satin bows on the wreaths; stone angels with lily crowns. For once life was stirring: jet beads and best dresses, starched collars, Sunday suits. Though lavatory creeper and stink weed tangled everywhere, they didn't count. Her giant's body went into the earth, but really she was up in the sky with gates of pearl and pavements of gold. All the niggling little things were left out — the pattern loomed large. They were heroes who mourned as pale petals were scattered by the wind, and it didn't matter about the gum trees and the raw red earth or the dusty road stretching ahead. The reins drooped in Papa's hands; even Mama stopped worrying over her stomach to look.

It was Australia, but the German words on the grave-stones were curly and tendrilled. Crystal knew what they said must be poetry: *Hier Ruhet in Gott ... Christus der ist Mein Leben* ... And there was a little lamb scabbed with lichen, and passion flowers carved on the cross. So many German girls had died: Mathilde, Wil-helmine, Anna ...

But then Rosa saw that Crystal had climbed down from the buggy and must call her back. She was a horrid older sister to have. Her thick slow voice was relentless; it ruined mysteries as it labelled, pinned down. Rosa spoke, and big things shrank to midget size. The gian-tess was merely a fat lady whose mortal remains would moulder away. Dying wasn't glorious, it was just paying nature's debt. And the grave was dark, the last retreat of all — though it was Papa who said those things, not Rosa. She was frowning over the map, asking him where they were. This time Papa answered; though he mostly chose to ignore her. Papa was the only thing that Rosa couldn't reduce. He was too crude and big for her: he was the only person Rosa loved.

But for once he had chosen to answer. He said they were somewhere near Arden Valley, and then the horse stopped nuzzling bleached grass and the buggy moved on. After the Hills, the country was strangely flat, so open; Crystal felt oddly exposed, surrounded by so much sky. And Mama's face was clenched again, for she was going to have a baby — it was something that couldn't be pretended away. Crystal longed for the cemetery's cool marble and wondered why their life must be like it; why Papa's eyes must turn dreamy. His dreaming eyes in his fierce set face were always a warn-ing that soon they'd be travelling; that they'd leave the soft safe Hills country, leave everything known.

Granpa's house, the mulberry tree by the gate, the lilies running down to the creek, the fruit garden, the wattles ...

It was shameful that they should set off like gipsies, not knowing where tomorrow would find them, or when they'd be back. The first few leavetakings Granpa stood stiff in the mulberry tree's shadow — it was true, for Rosa remembered. His beard was frothy, he had small feet and hands; his God was different to Papa's.

Granpa had been a Wesleyan; once Mama was, too. But then she met Papa: then she was nothing. He had hands like roots and she was little and weak. She was silly, sentimental then, with velvet ribbon in her hair. She was ladylike, singing in the choir in shot silk. She had a shepherdess hat, kitten eyes.

Somewhere among the apple trees she met him. He came slinking, skulking into her life, with his great twisted hands, his ragged beard. He always dressed in black city clothes; he looked like a gloomy prophet walking in the orchards. He was a preacher, they whispered in chapel.

And Reverend was a softie; he shook the stranger's hand, he invited him into the pulpit. That Sunday, Daisy Nelson felt on fire. Her cheeks burned, she was so proud. Her mouth kept trembling, she couldn't stop smiling. For she loved him — in the orchard he said nothing they did was wrong.

The congregation stirred, expectant, but to begin with Ebenezer Sparks disappointed. He'd never convert multitudes with his voice. He was mild, wistful, as he spoke of a nursery-rhyme land of milk and honey; of souls washed white and sheep at rest in the fold. But suddenly his voice changed, the words were different. There were no more realms of endless day; no pastures

5

green and fair. Instead, the mountains were thirsty, they started to pant; the oceans were full of snapping teeth; there were paths of death, dreadful shades. And He wasn't Gentle Jesus. He was a man with pierced hands, a broken body, and He hung on the cross and it was vile — the agony, the fear. It was a devil, now, who stood in the pulpit, and he was glaring like a tiger cat and a poison swamp came out of his mouth. It was sickening what his voice made them see. England stopped being Home with robin redbreast and the Queen. Ragged women swarmed about as filthy as swine; children were put to work in the mines. Men stole because they starved, and there was a man who stole a silk handkerchief, a pair of sugar tongs, and was banished from his homeland for ever. And, dear God, it was Sunday chapel with roast and mint sauce to follow, but he had to start off about the convict ships, and it was years ago, and they'd each put sixpence in for collection, they'd paid their way, they didn't deserve it — not the evil quivering off his voice like daggers that cut, that sliced at the bonds that bound them together as fellow Christian travellers with nothing worse than Heaven before them. All the respectable veneer of living safe for years fell away. His voice cut them off from the snug certainties — nothing was sure, they'd stopped being part of a family. Each was an individual, alone in a hostile world. They shivered as if they were naked; his voice made them feel and see … and you saw the felons in their rags stamped with arrows and then they stopped being *them*, then they were *you*. The lash came down until you were reduced to a gibbering animal, and there was the treadmill and the triangle and your back was a red shirt and all the man had been flogged out of you; now you were merely something of the nature of a spaniel dog …

The flowers and fruits on the ladies' bonnets quivered as this one and that started leaving. Even Reverend was up on his feet. And then a better bit happened. The Nelson girl, that little dimpled thing, came down from the choir. Whoever would have thought it? — she had linked the blasphemer's arm.

Daisy Nelson wasn't seen in Appleton for years. When she came back she was almost a stranger. Mrs Sparks didn't frizz her hair; there were no follow-me-lads streamers on her bonnets. She was a sad creature, quiet and creeping, with a cough in her voice and worried hands.

She had married him, it was a pity. He was a scoundrel who had no shame. For he stole her away, then brought her back, so he might live in her father's house. What she saw in him, Appleton couldn't guess. His face was seamed; he looked old (though not as old as her father, that old man, white-bearded, who used to ride the white Arab horse). He stood crooked in his black city clothes. He never wore flannels and moleskins like other men — not even when he was out stripping wattle.

Once Nelson's five acres were planted with vines, and it used to be called the vineyard. There were a lot of vines round that part of the Hills once, but there came a time when they weren't worth anything; there was no money in them, so people let them die. The wattles grew up in their place. In springtime Ebenezer Sparks would set to work and strip them.

He cut the wattles down with an axe. It was the time of the year when the sap was rising, and so usually the bark came loose without much trouble. He'd knock up a stand from saplings, to hold the wattle butt steady, then start tapping with the back of his tommyhawk. Up and down he'd tap, round and round, until the bark split

7

itself and came off nicely. His hands went black as coal (it was the tannin coming out), but he worked quickly, neatly. He folded the bark into bundles, all the same size, and tied them with string.

The wattle bark was sold to a factory at Beauville that made leather. Beauville was an inner suburb of the city near the Hills; a region of brick-kilns and gasometers, breweries and ropeworks. Here, the river flowed sluggishly, its banks lined with the factories of fell-mongers and wool-scourers, soapmakers and tanners.

And Crystal had these dreams, they were awful. The factory chimneys belched smoke; there was a smell like the slimy scent, green and furry, when the flowers had died in the vase. This smell clung to her dreams and stick people walked about shivering; it was winter when Mama had her cough and under her pinny her belly stuck out, but the new baby always died. And she wasn't that old, Papa was years and years older, but he stayed big and strong in his tight black clothes. His beard had hardly any silver; it sprang like fine wire from the lines in his face and his animal teeth laughed in a zigzag.

After Daisy's father died, Nelson's was a wilderness. The garden went wild. The rose stems curled up like whips, morning glory tangled everywhere, the lilies spread further along the creek.

Mr Nelson had been inspector of codlin moth. He'd have turned in his grave if he could've seen his apple trees now. The old codlin was having a field day. And there was scab and shot-hole in the apricots; curl leaf on the peach. And aphis and gumming; black spot and mildew. Ebenezer Sparks wandered, smiling, among the trees as peaches fell with soft thuds. The grass was clotted with decaying fruit threaded with ants; there was a sick jammy stink, clouds of midges. Yet he merely stared at the sky as if its blueness surprised him; he preached mumbled sermons to birds, lay dead-man stretched in the grass. And then, without warning, he'd come awake to the blight about him. Too late, he'd be working in a fever: shaking dry sulphur at the trees while the dew was on them, spraying with urine water and tobacco-wash; scattering ashes round roots, slitting bark.

He was as mad as a penny watch. A spell in the fruit garden guaranteed that he'd soon be seen stumbling home, reeking of whisky.

It was a favourite topic at tea-parties — how Daisy Sparks could bear him near her. The ladies cocked their fingers and dunked their ginger-nuts genteely as they thought it over. It was delicious to ponder — too horrid: how she could bear to submit. He was a brute. And she had Rosa already when she came back to the Hills, though Crystal wasn't born until years later. But before Crystal, and after, a baby was always on the way, though she always suffered a mishap — either that, or it hardly lived to breathe. Poor soul. But it was a mercy, really. What life was it for a child, all that gipsying about? And him for a father — what a fate.

Crystal hated him, but he could even be nice. He was all right when he sat in his chair under the grape-vine. Granpa had planted it: it went along the verandah at the back. At the back of the house in summer it was all grapes hanging down. It was so pretty, with the fretted leaves and the purple bunches, sort of dusty.

Papa would sit there and smoke. The tobacco smell was like perfume. Sometimes Mama came out and sat down, too, and Crystal felt that she was part of a family, just like everyone else. She could forget Papa's queerness, how he was somehow more animal than man. It was his skin being rough, the fierceness of his beard, the hairs that bristled from his nostrils and hung in small tassels from his ears and crept out from under his shirt-cuffs — it was something cowed about him. Though that was absurd: Papa was fierce.

Crystal yearned to belong; she wanted a life that was proper. She was a Nelson, not a Sparks. She *had* to hate him for he'd come, elemental as a storm, to ruin their lives.

Mama had betrayed Granpa and the life he'd given her; even now she kept on betraying herself. She spoke of that other Daisy calmly, in an interested voice — of her African monkey muff, her sandalwood fan — as if she'd been an exotic chance acquaintance who'd passed through her life. That Daisy was a curiosity of 1870 who'd ceased to exist, and Mama didn't mourn her demise.

In any case, the dress with pagoda sleeves and the Greek key pattern in braid round its skirt had only been put on for best. Life had mostly meant a sacking apron and Daisy Nelson playing at skivvy. Granpa had kept cows — it was Daisy who milked them, and humped buckets of sour milk to the pigs. In winter she must trudge through muck, ankle-deep; and what about that time when she acted as scarecrow?

Crystal didn't want to listen, she knew that Mama fibbed. She was so besotted she did it out of pity: downgraded her life until it approached the level of his.

It was Papa who'd been pecked at by birds, who'd trudged through swamps, and fought his way past thickets of thorn bush. Some grasses had an edge like a knife, fern stalks were spears, certain vines were armed with sharp hooks. He'd been a hunted thing that had crouched and crawled; that had hidden and tunnelled and twisted. He'd been lost in a merciless world where frantic shadows pressed close and night was a black cape come to smother him away until leaves let in blobs of sunshine that trembled and merged to form a giant eye of God. Papa was an animal down in the darkness and somehow God's eye had found him and had burned him with its cold ardour for life; even as it guided him, saved him, through jungles of bushland, networks of ravines. In and out of valleys, over breakneck rocks — a cruel God was with Papa all the way.

It was another dream, one of the worst. Night after night Crystal saw him like that. Though on a good day when he smoked under the vine arbour, or whistled as he flung wheat at the fowls, it seemed silly to picture him so. He was her father. He had an English voice, he read from the big Bible. It was only occasionally that he came home drunk. It wasn't him, truly, in the dream. He wasn't that savage thing, hunted and hiding.

But what part of England did he come from, why had he left if for Australia? Papa's past made a mystery that Crystal couldn't solve. When she'd asked him about it, he wouldn't answer.

Sometimes it seemed that the dream wasn't so fanciful. Once Crystal saw Papa with his shirt off. She never forgot. It might even have been a thorn bush that had torn him so terribly, that had given him those marks on his back. He was scored from the nape of his neck to his waist. It was ugly; much uglier than his stained hands when he stripped wattle bark. The skin of his back looked dead: Papa had a back like leather.

•••

11

After a bout of drinking he'd read the Bible. His voice would drone on and, to begin with, they'd mime pious attention; then, after a while, they crept from the room.

But one day in autumn his voice trailed off, and they knew they'd be going away. The Bible verse stayed unfinished, for his eyes were dreamy. It didn't matter that Rosa was sorting the washing, or that Crystal had set out for school. The whites and coloureds stayed muddled together and Crystal must turn back on the road. It was nearly time for Mama to have the baby, but he didn't even care about that. They were his to do with as he pleased.

So life meant riding in the buggy again, the old horse pulling them along. Rosa sat up in front beside Papa (travelling, he was hers, she didn't want to share him); Mama and Crystal huddled together at the back.

Though they set off when the sky was blue, it didn't seem like an adventure. Home was left behind. They were birds of passage, rolling stones. They had the tent and the rugs and the things in the baskets. It was madness that Mama should journey in her condition.

Mrs Thorn had thought so, she'd tried to hold her back, but Mama had pushed off her arms. The Thorns had the house up the road. Their orchard was a model one, for Mr Thorn pruned on sound lines, he thinned out his fruit, and spraying was never neglected. In his garden, weeds were conspicuous by their absence; he grew strawberries and loganberries; he had cows and a pig.

It would be the Thorns who saw to Papa's fowls, who'd guard the house from intruders. Mrs Thorn was expecting, too. But her baby would live; it would be dimpled and pink. Mama's babies were puny, after a few days they died.

Travelling, Papa was happy. His face looked serene; he whistled as the horse led them on. They were still in the Hills, but the country had ceased being familiar. They travelled strange roads, they saw different things.

Instead of apple trees there were cherries, plums, pears; instead of Appleton's little shops and houses they saw a jam factory, a butter factory, flour mills and chaff mills. They passed gloomy villas where surely murders had been done; and now the tree trunks were as black as the earth that was crusted with sad sepia leaves, for bushfires had been here before them; and then the country was all England, there were soft sappy greens, and they saw the house on the corner of the doiley with its hollyhock garden. And here was the Inebriates' Retreat; there, the Scenic Hotel.

For a time they kept being safe. Crystal relaxed, for it seemed that the Hills went on for ever and Mama was smiling, the weather stayed fine. At night it was snug in the tent; and a camping holiday was in fashion; and probably they wouldn't go far — even now, he was perhaps deciding to turn back.

It was playing a game of pretending. Papa was a gentleman jingling money in his pocket as he stopped at the baker's, the grocer's, the dairy. And he went away with his gun, he came back with a rabbit, and Mama hummed as she filled their plates with stew.

The country was nearly all a garden. They passed orchards and strawberry beds; vegetable gardens, flower gardens. The stream from the waterfall slid away in a silver ribbon. There were gullies of maidenhair fern; hazelnut and walnut glens.

The road wound in serpentine curves; it corkscrewed down to deep valleys, then rose in a dizzy rush at the summit. They breathed in mountain air *par excellence*, and saw the *élite* of the city's summer mansions.

But soon the houses were left behind and the country had changed. The only hills, now, were far ahead, purply dark. They were sinister, Crystal never wanted to reach them. Though the country about them was as bad.

They crossed a great plain strewn with the tormented shapes of dead trees. Here and there the gums still stood, but even they resembled gaunt monsters. And there were stumps of trees, too, and dried furze bushes, prickly and dusty. The gums were a dull silver-grey; they looked like petrified trees, trees that were carved from stone. The plain was dun-coloured; it was like crossing the rumpled pelt of a giant animal. The land lay low under a high white sky. And far away were those bruised purple hills. Papa was another man, now. He sat stiffly, he didn't dream.

The sun was so hot; it even sought them out in the patch of scrub. But Papa didn't care, his teeth were laughing as he fashioned the humpy of woven boughs. It was as if they weren't there, he didn't see them. He was a man alone as he crept between the gum trees to find the waterhole, to catch the rabbit in his trap (this time he killed it with his hands). Mama made the same stew, but he didn't bother to eat genteel — he didn't hold his beard back while he took a mouthful.

But the Johnny cakes he cooked for breakfast next morning were good. They were made in the same way as damper, and their other name was devils on the coals.

Then they were off again. They came to the cemetery and watched the giantess's funeral and then went on down the road. Arden Valley was somewhere ahead. Mama was screwing up her face. Crystal felt scared, for it might mean that the baby was coming.

And, ever after, the place would mean a nightmare that Crystal couldn't pretend away. But, to begin with, Arden Valley was perfect; it meant a long depression, a hollow lying between hills. Down there, everything was gay and green. Crystal knew that when they reached bottom and looked up, the sky would be a deeper blue, the sun would shine brighter. It was like entering another world; it was like the domains and gardens of some splendid estate in the best part of Europe. It was the world of a fairy-tale, fleshed out, and there were goose-girls with flaxen hair; gabled houses with rainbow gardens. There were foreign names on the shops, and the baker's was best of all. There were gingerbread men, honey biscuits dusted with sugar. And there were hay-stacks and fat sheep and spotted cows. And more vines turning gold — more and more.

Arden Valley meant sherry and port wine; burgundy, claret, champagne. The slopes of its hills were covered with grape-vines. So great was the care with which they'd been planted, that scarcely a single plant was to be seen irregularly placed.

There weren't any grapes: Crystal saw frilly leaves. They were greeny-gold, turning copper — there were bronze tints creeping into the leaves. Some vines were neat; others tangled, trailed. Some were just skeleton stumps.

Vintage was over. A few weeks ago the vineyards had been full of girls, their sun-bonnets adorned with flowers. The grape-pickers gathered the juicy bunches with nimble fingers. Basket after basket was filled and handed on to the waggons which, in a continuous stream, passed to and fro to the cellars.

The Valley had been settled by Germans, Lutheran refugees from religious persecution. They brought with them to the new country the carved cedar table, the old white rocking-chair; and feather mattresses, spittoons, violins; and memories of wolf-haunted forests, snow-storms and mists. It was as if a piece of Silesia or Saxony had been uprooted, transported by sailing ship and then bullock dray and ox cart, then set down, intact, among the gum trees. Soon the landscape had changed to suit them — the men with meerschaum pipes and velvet caps, the girls driving their geese homeward with long sticks, the women with snowy bundles of laundry on their heads. They built the gabled houses, the lattice-windowed shops, the high-spired church. Green pyramids of larches, walnut trees and spruce firs grew from the seeds they brought with them in their baggage. The greatest change came when the Valley's sandy loam soil proved a vigneron's paradise. Mr Arden came there, then, to give the Valley his name.

And suddenly Crystal saw a castle. Its massive blue-stone front rose out of the vines, there was a tower inset with a clock. There wasn't a moat or a drawbridge, but the windows were diamond-paned, the wall had a crenellated top. And Crystal saw skinny chimneys, so tall, and it was then that the nightmare began — Arden Valley started being a place that would suit cruel step-mothers and wild beasts. All at once it was the castle where the wicked fairy lived who changed the maidens into birds. Her chamber was hung with their cages, and the clock started chiming and Mama jerked forward; she was squirming, as if she tried to escape. And there was a smell drifting everywhere, so queer. It was rich and fruity; it was nasty, nice. It was a smell with a hint of cess-pit, but it had nothing to do with Beauville — the Beauville scent was different. Mama was clutching her hanky in a little ball. Her mouth was stretched; she was hideous, like a monkey in pain.

It was Rosa who made Papa see; who made him carry her away. Now there was blond grass about them, satiny, silky, and a smell of liquorice from the fennel. Leaves glittered glassily; they were in the grass at the side of the road. The sun kept teasing it — the grass glistened silver, it went pinky, then gold; it was bobbled and plumed and tasselled. One day Crystal would have a dress with bobbles like that — a dress of stamped velvet with a waterfall skirt. She didn't want to see, to hear; to be where Mama moaned. The bleached grass tangled stiffly, and then Papa had carried her from it. The castle had disappeared; they had come to a pair of gates.

Behind the fence of iron spears there was a park. The grass was plushy, there was a line of pine trees that nibbled in inky zigzags at the sky. And though Mama still moaned in Papa's arms, the fairy-tale turned soothing again, the wild beasts jumped back. Instead of lions and tigers, the park was speckled with deer. They had twitchy mouths and velvet noses, antlers like candelabra. And there was a hedge of rosemary and a little garden and Papa's boots trod everywhere; they trampled the pansies and violets, the cherry-pie and dwarf sunflowers. He carried her past the shivery aspen tree and the thicket of Belladonna lilies; the ropes of ivy, the honeysuckle that dangled in festoons. He didn't care about anything — only Mama — as he passed the great-winged resurrection angel with a star in its crown and a dove on the tip of its finger. He laid her down by the mausoleum.

Then he ran and ran until he turned small. He ran up the drive that stretched between pines to the house. It was white, far away, like a doll's house.

Mama lay beside the tomb looking up at the dove on the angel's finger. Rosa was bending over her, doing things — Rosa owned Mama, now, and Crystal didn't care. For they were both fools — Mama was as much a lackbrain as Papa. She was mad to have started out travelling, to have ended up writhing on some stranger's lawn. She ruined the angel's calm face; made a mockery of death's perfect trappings. Proper people gave birth in bedrooms on a mackintosh sheet, with fountain syringe, hot water bottle, carbolic, olive oil and an abundant supply of soft rags to hand.

A miracle happened: she had all those things. And a carriage rattled down the drive and came back with a doctor. His voice sounded expensive; his hands smelled of Windsor soap. Mama had been plucked from the grass to lie inside Arden House.

Crystal had been put in the pink room. Moss roses latticed the walls; there were muslin curtains, a lacy bedspread. The brass bed was wonderfully knobbed, there was an embroidered splash-back to the washstand. But the dressing-table, muslin-skirted, was best — it was covered with treasures: silver combs and brushes, cut glass scent bottles, a fat pincushion incrusted with beads. The looking-glass was a Psyche sort, that swung. It was draped in muslin, too: the girl it reflected was a bride.

Crystal saw a foxy sort of girl, very pale ... foxy, because of her narrow pointed face; because of her hair.

Always, until now — until she looked in the mirror at Arden House — red hair had been something to be ashamed of. It was so crinkly; such a frizz bush. "Carrots," the Appleton boys would jeer as she passed, and: "Ginger."

But Arden House made everything different. This girl was a bride in a cobweb veil. What lovely hair, what a beautiful young creature. Then Crystal blushed, and the mirror-girl jumped back, for someone tapped at the door.

It was the lady who'd bade them enter the house. She had black crackly skirts and a cameo; she was perfectly prim and precise, rigid and frigid; she was a lady who might have been a duchess, when she spoke lesser ladies scuttled.

One of them stood beside her, now, with two jugs. Crystal admired her cap and turn-down collar, her cuffs and lace-trimmed apron. But when she stepped forward she wasn't so pleasant. For the jugs splashed hot and cold into the bowl on the washstand and then the lesser lady pounced. The duchess came to help her and Crystal struggled, but in a trice they had her out of her dress. She shivered with shame as they sneered at her knickers, as they washed her in every secret place. They scrubbed and rubbed until she shone, and dug at her fingernails. Her head felt on fire from all their brushing and combing, but after the carnation talcum it was thrilling, Crystal ceased snivelling, for they disguised her in another girl's clothes. There was even a pair of swanskin stays; there were several petticoats, tickly with starch, and on top went a white embroidered frock. Now Crystal's stockings were silk; her slippers had ribbon rosettes.

The lady with the cameo led her away, the passage

went on for ever. It twisted, it turned, and there were a great many doors. But the lady knew which one to stop at.

The room was dim, it was full of strange things. In the darkness they seemed to swim together, to blend: the curiously carved cabinets, the Chinese bamboo chairs; the fierce stuffed lions' heads, the Polar bear rug. There were gilt clocks, bronze statuettes, shell flowers under glass. It was a collector's room, and on the couch was a row of dolls. They sat stiffly, like frozen children. The one with Goldilocks hair and paperweight eyes was almost as big as Crystal. There was a baby doll, chubby and dimpled; a sailor doll with a Jack Tar straw hat. Beside him was the old lady — even bigger than Goldilocks and so comical, despite her sombre dress. She had a podgy Queen Victoria face, bulgy eyes, and a mouth that squeezed tight then stretched as wide as the mouth of the ventriloquist's doll. And she was mechanical in other ways, too, for she was nodding and beckoning, she almost looked real. And then Crystal only wanted to be gone, to be where things were ordinary, understandable. For it wasn't a doll at all, it was a little old lady dressed in black. She was smiling, holding out her arms.

The duchess was still there, she pushed Crystal forward, and the old lady moved up on the sofa. Now Crystal sat between her and the sailor boy (he had an anchor on his collar, a toy yacht on his lap). It was so cosy sitting close to the old lady's plump body that Crystal stopped being scared. She was the dearest old thing. Her complexion was of that peachy kind that looked as if it were preserved in sugar. When she spoke, her tongue seemed to suck on each word — all her words sounded syrupy, sweet.

One instant she was a grown-up, saying: "Thank you, Rudd, that will be all until I ring for tea," the next she was a little girl, giggling at Crystal, saying: "Will you be my friend?" It was a game, and Crystal wanted to laugh. But she didn't, for the old lady was Mrs Arden and she was sad because her loved one had died.

And Crystal learned that the tower and the diamond panes meant wine cellars, not a castle; and that the fruity smell tinged with cess-pit was to do with making wine. Mrs Arden sighed and said the Arden Valley Winery was famous, and once Mr Arden had owned it, and all the vineyards, too. But one day the Angel of Death came to claim him, and Mrs Arden hadn't known what to do. For, while hubby lived, she'd been a tee-totaller who'd suffered in silence, even though there was a wine called Tears of Christ. So it seemed best, after the funeral, to have the wine grapes grafted to currants. But, really, she couldn't decide. In the end it seemed better to sell.

So someone else owned the winery, now, and — remembering — Mrs Arden started crying. For she'd loved hubby dearly; it was why she'd wear widow's weeds for life.

Deepest mourning wasn't unbecoming. Though Mrs Arden's bombazine gown was shrouded in crape, she allowed herself pin-tucks and double ruffles and a fig-leaf apron mazed with jet. She was prickly with brooches and lockets and rings; buttons and necklaces and pins — all the best sorts for grieving, the most dole-ful, inset with death's heads and sad weeping willows, solemn mottoes and snippets of hair. Love-ribbon fluttered from her widow's cap as well as a nun's veiling streamer. The longer your cuffs were, the more it showed you cared — Mrs Arden's came up to her elbows.

The sweet voice dropped low; it went purry, caressing, as the witchetty-grub mouth nuzzled close. The face was so pink and quilted, the faded blue eyes so moist. Mrs Arden murmured, and her secrets teased Crystal's body as much as her ear. That mournful bodice was curiously pleasant to lean on, as Mrs Arden confided.

And Crystal learned that underneath the widow's weeds, inside the roly-poly body, was a secret little German girl named Clara. Oh, how lonely she was; oh, how she longed for a playmate. Mrs Arden's syrupy voice was a child's, pouting and lisping, as she told how once Clara had lived in a modest house in the Valley and her mama wore a cap like an egg-shell and baked resurrection pie; her papa carved Baby Jesus in the manger and He went up on the fir tree with the gingerbread animals, the tinsel stars. And Clara had girl friends: Emma, Amalie, Mathilde ... they were always together, doing things: someone was getting married, so they sat at the big table sorting feathers for a marriage-bed quilt; and there were picnics with potato salad, salted herrings; and Christmas meant honey cake and a sugar pig. It was meant to go on for ever — Clara and her girl friends and cuckoo clocks, lace curtains — but one day Mr Arden saw her and he loved her, he married her, he snatched her away to live with him in Arden House. Once Clara had made a trip on a ship, all the way from the old world to the new; but this was an even farther journeying. Clara swapped her girl friends for a China silk dress, a bonnet with plumes — she did it happily, so easily, but once it was done she found herself stranded. Being Mrs Arden made you different from everyone; made you foreign, even to yourself.

Crystal had set out from Appleton with Mama and

Papa and Rosa; with them, she'd entered Arden House where, to begin with, only Mama's delicate condition had been of interest. Perhaps the little stranger was still on its way; perhaps it had already departed (the baby would die, they always did). But what ever had happened — was happening — Mama no longer mattered. The only Sparks of import, now, was Crystal.

She was going to be Mrs Arden's. She would wear the starched dress, sleep in the pink room for ever. It would be a sure way of sidestepping Papa and Beauville.

Mrs Arden said she was feeling peckish, that it was time for Rudd to bring them their tea. She rang a bell, and spoke once more of Mr Arden. Of how, when he died, he'd gone into the Arden mausoleum, and she'd made him a garden. Mrs Arden had known her Language of Flowers and had planted rosemary for remembrance and violets for faithfulness. She swished back the curtains and beckoned Crystal to join her. In the distance was Mr Arden's grave, and dwarf sunflower meant "your devout adorer" and honeysuckle, "bond of love" ...

But Crystal wasn't listening; she was looking — but not at the mausoleum. On the occasional table stood a series of small gilt frames.

Mrs Arden collected children. Each frame held a photograph of a child's face. They were all dear little girls — all except one.

The little boy didn't simper or pretend innocence. He was pretty, certainly, with his melting eyes, his pursed rosebud mouth, but there was a jeer in that mouth, something knowing, unchildlike in those eyes.

Crystal started, for Mrs Arden had turned from the window to catch her peering at the photos. But the old lady didn't seem to mind. She stretched out her hand

and took up the framed little boy. "Naughty Val," she said dreamily, studying the child's face. Her voice was sweeter than ever, as: "Ah, my little love, my Valentine," she crooned.

Then, without warning, she threw him down. She was still smiling, that was the worst thing, as she trampled the boy's face beneath her shoe.

Next morning, remembering in the pink room, teatime was muddled, like a dream. It had gone on and on, until it surely merged with supper, and sometimes they talked — mostly they ate. Mrs Arden's lips were worms, wriggly and shiny, as they closed on pickled cucumbers, pickled fish. Everything tasted nice, but so odd. Despite willow pattern and lace doilies and Rudd's frigid face, teatime was somehow perverse. Nothing was merely nice, merely toothsome. At the back of each bite — even the sweetest — was a lingering hint of spice.

Crystal ate queer dark breads and delicacies of the sausage kind, and Mrs Arden devoured everything pickled, and then they stopped for a bit and played with the dolls. They were Clara and Crystal, then, and who'd imagine that the baby doll had a head that swivelled? — it was done by pulling a string. The doll's head turned round and under the frilly bonnet was a new face that didn't smile. This time Baby was crying, she showed a horrid red tongue.

They ate braided pastries bursting with dried fruits; they drank something steaming that smelled of cinnamon and cloves. Mrs Arden's words slurred as she said hot toddy wasn't a sin; toddy didn't count as wine, oh no. Crystal's head felt lolling and heavy. The dolls crowded round and the baby doll cried worse — her voice was tinny, tiny, it seemed to come from a long way off.

Then Crystal must have fallen asleep and someone must have carried her off to bed. When she woke it was morning in the pink room and, despite last night, she was hungry. She supposed breakfast would be brought on a tray. But nothing happened, no one came. Crystal sat up in bed in another girl's nightgown and sunshine came in at the window, the nightie was of finest nainsook, but she felt miserable, cold.

But it was absurd to imagine herself abandoned. She'd put on the starched frock and find Clara. But the frock and all the other finery of yesterday had vanished. In their place was a drab print dress, a grubby petticoat ...

And the knickers were patched, but Crystal pulled them on — she had to, for they were hers. She huddled into the shabby clothes and laced up the down-at-heel boots.

She thought she knew which way to go. But the passage somehow led her astray, and one door looked the same as another.

Crystal had begun by searching for Clara; she ended up exploring the house. She peered into rooms where dust drapes made ghost shapes, and into rooms where there was nothing at all. From behind a door she heard a voice — it was the squirming voice Papa used when he prayed. She walked fast until she'd left it behind. She came to a narrow flight of stairs.

Now she was up in the house so high; it was a different world up there. Creaking boards took the place of carpet; it was dim, even darker than Mrs Arden's room. It was like walking in a cage, a maze, and there were people in the house, but she'd dodged Papa's voice

— now she was alone, she couldn't find anyone. Yet there were whispers all about her. She was high in the house, above the tops of the trees, close to flap-winged birds and winds that made a noise like the sea.

Then a door sprang open. Light spilled out and he stood there: a pretty boy dressed for a party in a Little Lord Fauntleroy suit. The black velvet, lace-collared, suited him perfectly. He had the dark gipsy ringlets, the right face: he was the boy in the photo.

Valentine's smile was welcoming as he took her hand. He was a nice little boy, small and babyish looking. She felt indignant that he should be here, alone.

The room was a nursery. Crystal had read Mrs Molesworth — the children in her books inhabited such places. She recognized the high brass fender, the rag rug, the rocking-chair with its patchwork cushions. There were regiments of soldiers in lead, a Noah's ark, a rocking-horse.

But Dobbin's scarlet nostrils were flaring, he had dangerous teeth. Crystal left off examining him, glad that Valentine called her away. Everything was magical, dreamlike. He'd been waiting for her, he'd known she was coming, and she sat beside him at the nursery table and wished he could have seen her as she'd been yester-day.

Then it was curious — she couldn't stop talking. She was telling him about the pink room, the white dress, her friendship with Clara. His eyes made her. And she told about living in Appleton, of travelling with Papa in the buggy. She left out the dreariness, the discomfort, she made it sound an adventure; she felt sorrier than ever for Valentine, immured in his nursery, as she des-cribed the different parts of the Hills. And she told him how travelling once before had meant Beauville and the factories, and how another time Papa had taken them to the coast. She mentioned waves and seaweeds and shells like fans and steeples, and then she didn't mean to — but she was telling him of the seagulls that swooped from the sky, that had run at her with fierce snapping beaks. Crystal had been scared, the beach was spoiled, and Valentine's rosebud mouth had disappeared, his smile was a crooked ripple, and she couldn't help it — but she was telling how she hated Papa and Beauville as much as the gulls. And she told about the stripes on his back — how under his shirt Papa's back was scarred, and how it was awful having Rosa for a sister, and how Mama's babies always died. And so would the latest, please God.

When she'd finished she felt strange, somehow empty. She had told him her secrets, he knew her nightmares, and she should have felt better, but she didn't. She'd betrayed them all and she didn't know who she was.

She felt lost and afraid, and Valentine smirked. But it was nonsense. He was so comely, with such winning ways, that surely he'd have innocence of soul. He was as good as the hero in the Sunday School prize book; he'd never shout "Carrots" like the Appleton boys, never pull off the fly's wings or cram baby frogs into a matchbox. She told him that she'd been invited to stay, and so he need never be lonely again.

The life they'd lead together was such a splendid imagining. In the white frock she'd be as immaculate as one of those Catholic girls got up as a Bride of Christ. And down by the front door a nigger boy with glass eyes held a lamp, a stuffed grizzly bear proffered a tea-tray. And there was plush furniture, velvet carpet, the scuttling ladies like black and white angels.

Crystal was happy, she was rosy with gladness. The

empty feeling had gone, she felt cosy inside. Excitement whipped her cheeks and coursed through her body to waggle at her fingertips, to fidget her toes. She jumped up from her chair, she couldn't keep still. Finding Valentine was like getting close to Granpa, and to Mama when she'd worn her pagoda sleeves.

She danced round the table like a mad thing, but he didn't applaud her performance. He sat very still, he might have been a boy turned to stone. And then he said she was vulgar and mincing; deceitful and cunning; a fool, an ignoramus. For it was a blackamoor not a nigger boy — it was a blackamoor torchère. And the grizzly bear's tray was for visiting-cards; they weren't angels but maids.

Now she was the statue and he walked round her — looking with his terrible eyes, wounding with his terrible words. This boy was old, much older than Crystal; she'd never known anyone so cruel. He'd tricked her with his childish pose; he was a pretender who'd prised out her secrets. "Do you really think she wants you?" he sneered. "Why, even if she meant her invitation; even if you stay at Arden House, it won't be for long. Mrs Arden is changeable; she can't resist a new plaything. As soon as Rudd told me of you I knew it would lead to this. But it doesn't mean a thing. There've been countless little girls come to Arden House already, but she tired of them, every one ..." And then on a whim she'd chosen a boy. Clara would never send him away. He was Valentine Arden, he'd never be anyone else.

He opened a door and led her into the night-nursery. There was a little white bed and pictures of people all over the walls. Everyone was washed very clean. There were lockets and pearls, lacy ruffles; nid-nodding

feathers and diamond crowns. The gentlemen wore
sashes and medals; their hair was parted very straight.

It was 1893 and Princess Vicky had married Fritz of
Prussia long ago, now she was the mother of Kaiser
William, but up on the wall she was still a child and
Valentine knew her pet name had been Pussette, and
that she did not cry at her christening. And this other
poppet was Princess Alice, extraordinarily good and
merry. And here was Princess Helena, remarkably en-
gaging; Princess Louise who was artistic; Princess
Beatrice, the Queen's youngest and well-beloved.

He passed over their brothers for a new set of princes
and one was Prince George, the other Prince Albert
Victor. They were sailor boys who'd visited Australia in
'81. After touring the cities the royal travellers had gone
out into the country where towns expressed their gratifi-
cation by erecting large triumphal arches. And they
descended copper mines and hunted kangaroos, and a
mounted policeman taught Prince George the whistling
call of the quail. But it was Albert Victor who interested
Valentine most. He'd turned into the Duke of Clarence,
he'd proposed to Princess May of Teck, then last year
he'd died.

Valentine's voice rambled on. He was telling how, all
those years ago, the Princes' tour had taken in Arden
Valley. There'd been the usual triumphal arch and an
excursion through the vines. And then Crystal was
listening, for surely he didn't say it? — but he did. Yes,
for what he said made a picture in her head and she saw
the girl with her charming gentle dignity — she was a
good girl, one saw at a glance. But the Prince saw her
first, and because of it the picture was shameful, but
Valentine kept talking and Crystal couldn't stop seeing
it: the girl in the vineyard and Albert Victor making a

detour and a prince always had his way and because of it a child was born.

Valentine had stopped being pretty. His face was blotched and wobbly, his voice rose higher as it came to the bit about how she was a delicate flower that could not bear the rough blasts of winter, the cold days of adversity. Beef-wine and jelly couldn't save her. "God bless my baby," she cried from her invalid couch, then breathed her last. Valentine would always remember. How she lay with her hands crossed over her breast, rosebuds scattered about her. How the organ played beautiful music, telling of mingled sorrow and hope eternal.

It was true, he hadn't made it up. He was different from the others at the orphanage and Mrs Arden wouldn't send him back. He would see her dead first.

And now the princes and princesses, the kings and queens were shut away with Mr and Mrs Noah. He'd shut the door, she was out in the passage, and somewhere the sun was shining, but here there were winds and swooping birds. The house shuddered and the passage was gloomy, it was sombre as Sunday and she had the hollow feeling, the sick nibble of fear. For the chapel bell rang and she never went; she was no one and it was dark, she'd never find the stairs; never have the dress whispery with starch, the dressing-table's cut glass. For a while they were hers, but it was all taken away and she'd never get over the hurt. It was dark in the passage and she wanted to run; she'd snap her fingers, call names at shadows. It was like wandering in London fog and she'd go there one day, see the royalty he spoke of, become the lady he didn't reckon she could be. She would have the dress, the scent bottle and a shiver ran through her at the long continuance of gloom. There weren't any pleasant gleams; it was horrid and the whispers had started. Somewhere there were people and there was a wild mournful crying, a low rumbling of laughter, and the flap-winged birds circled lower until one had somehow got inside her — it was under her bodice, it tickled against her, it fluttered in a frenzy for there were footsteps now, too.

Someone tagged her down the passage. It would be the black man who was always waiting; it would be the big white lady, all white and cold. She tried to walk faster; she thought she saw the stairs. And now it was upon her, but then it went past her. And it wasn't black man, white lady. Valentine had heard the voices, too, they'd drawn him into the passage. Downstairs there were people and a baby was crying, Mrs Arden laughed worse.

Now Crystal had caught him up, she stood beside him at the open door. It was a bedroom and Mama fell back on the pillow as Mrs Arden snatched Baby away. It was so small as it spilled from its shell-stitch cocoon and Mrs Arden kept laughing, she barked like a whole kennel of dogs. The shawl came undone, Baby fell on to the bed. It was red in the face, a wrinkled curiosity, but Mrs Arden fondled it with maudlin fondness, she talked without cease in foolish strain. She called it little fairy, dainty morsel, and puffed her cheeks at its high-coloured face. Baby cried louder and kicked at her with skimpy legs, but she called it poppet, little sweetheart and Crystal saw a foot like a wrinkled flower petal and each toe was a dot with a speck of pearly nail and the foot was so perfect — but it was a midget, a dwarf.

Crystal hated, she didn't care, as Mama protested weakly. But Mrs Arden wouldn't stop. She pulled off the health flannel layers, she dressed it all over again. There was a silk robe and sash, a cap like a sunflower, a coral necklace for luck.

Valentine ran forward, but Mrs Arden wouldn't see him, just as she wouldn't see Crystal. She only wanted Baby — it was Baby who'd stay with her and Mama sucked at air, she was as pale as death. Mrs Arden stood in for her. She was a picture of maternal love as she started on a go-to-sleep song. "Is the wild bird a little shy tonight?" she sang. "She will be calmer by and by ..."

Then everything was in dire confusion. Valentine sprang, and Mrs Arden stopped playing at angel mother. He pulled at her skirts until she saw him, and a sullen look drifted on to her face. He was wicked, she said. He'd broken her heart; he'd bring down her grey hairs with sorrow to the grave. She didn't want him, she was sending him back.

Her words turned Valentine into a fury. His face was a sharp mask, glitter-eyed, as he kicked and clawed and tore. The baby's robe was in rags, the sunflower cap was ripped to shreds. It was a poor pink thing, nodding and shaking with an imbecile aspect, and the sun knocked a warning at the window, dust motes flew, the room was full of yellow light. The child would be crushed; it was all puckered and pinched. Mama cried out again and Crystal felt confused. For it was a monster — it would be a kindness to let them maul it away. Yet Mama wanted it and so Crystal saved it. They were mad things, but she braved them as she jerked its squirming body free.

But though the prize had been carried off, to lay sheltered by Mama's arms, their grappling didn't cease. Valentine threw himself at Mrs Arden's prickly bodice; he pummelled her death's heads and solemn mottoes. A weeping willow brooch flew off, the floor was crusted with bugle beads and jet.

He scratched at her cheeks until they burned scarlet as flags. Love-ribbon fluttered, her eyes flew back, but her bleeding face stayed soft and smiling, her voice came in choking gasps of pleasure. But she was saying it was wicked, so wicked. For God hated lying. God said all liars should have their part in the lake that burned with fire and brimstone. Satan was the father of lies; those who were guilty of lying were that wicked one's children.

Papa said the same sort of thing when he'd been drinking; the queer Bible names slipped just as easily off his tongue, though Papa's favourites were Moses who made the bush burn and Joshua for whom the sun stood still. Mrs Arden's Bible people were different — they were Gehazi and Ananias and Sapphira, and the last two were struck dead and Gehazi was made into a leper. She told their stories so well that Crystal saw them stretched out in their grave-clothes; saw his leper spots, white as snow. And it was God who did it, and He'd done it for their lies. God had punished them and He'd do it to Valentine, too.

Now Mrs Arden had started on a new story, one you wouldn't find in the Bible. Her voice sounded comforting, but Valentine covered his ears to shut it out.

Yet it was his story she told. But in Mrs Arden's telling the facts were different. It wasn't a prince who did the shameful thing to the girl in the vines. In Mrs Arden's version it was just any man who pulled up her skirts — any man, every man, the girl didn't care who.

And she was a factory girl with a fringe and an emancipation bodice. She was the Valley whore running wild under a hatload of scarlet feathers. She was as bad as Jezebel who was gobbled by dogs to end up just a skull, a pair of feet and the palms for her hands.

It was Jezebel's punishment and the whore got one, too. She didn't die in a scatter of rosebuds; it wasn't like poetry with feet moving gently along corridors and her name uttered in low hushed tones. No one mourned her, no one cared. Only the smell had given her away — that, and the baby's crying. The stink of death came creeping from her hovel and they found Valentine clinging to life beside her.

And what was it like to be down there on the floor? To be Valentine with his nose pressed into the hearthrug, tears sinking into warm Turkey red? He'd curled himself tight, he was a glossy velvet ball. Poor poor thing — Little Fauntleroy, so black and white, for a while so still, then shaking out the terrible sobs. But her voice continued, relentless.

... and at night from his barred bed he wandered an enchanted wood. The sadness of being no one stopped mattering. It was the orphanage, but strange trees struck root and through his private forest a prince came riding, fairy horns blew, and Valentine was swept up in the heady chase as he hunted out a family of his own. Oh Mama, Mama — and he snipped another princess, he pinned her to the wall and went on believing, and one day she came — an old lady in mourning, like the Queen. She knew who he was, she picked him out straight away ...

If he couldn't win her by love he'd do it by hate (but secretly, so no one guessed). It was his house, not hers. He knew it from cellar to attic; he loved all its contents — the more he had, the safer he'd be. Mrs Arden hoarded dolls; Valentine's collection would baffle description. It would be a unique assortment, a vast display.

He knew tricks, for his sodden eyes turned dry and Fauntleroy was so natty, so perfectly neutral, while the old lady was dishevelled, her garments gave a terrifying impression of slipping off. She was supposed to be mistress but she wouldn't even do for a kitchen romp, for no decent servant would sanction it and certainly not Rudd. The housekeeper's vinegar countenance pushed passion back; a north-easterly blew, winter reigned. Mrs Arden was vulgar and Clara knew it, she whimpered an apology and would Valentine be her sweetheart, her special friend for the ensuing year? Oh please, she begged — a little German girl, lonely. And her mouth was crumbed with honey cake, a lace curtain billowed, a clock cuckooed the hour. She was amorous, sentimental, as she reached for Little Fauntleroy. She soothed his love-locks and said he would stay for ever. He was crushed to her mourning; their different blacks mingled until they might have been one.

But Valentine wasn't fooled. He knew her "for ever" would only last until her gaze strayed to another child. And he stared over her shoulder at the Sparkses as if he meant to get them to heart. They were a family who'd come trespassing into his life, they'd almost succeeded in stealing his future. They were representatives of all those pretenders who'd come to Arden House before him; of any other usurpers who might try to come after. He would never forget: the foxy girl with her cloud of red hair, the baby and the big sister come into the room

35

to gather her up, the old man who was lifting the mother from the bed. Mrs Sparks's feet dangled down from her virgin's nightgown and her hair was a plaited snake. She was pale as a dying woman; she was a Sparks who didn't count. But the man wrapped her in his coat so carefully, and Valentine knew what was under his shirt and it was like having Ebenezer Sparks in his power. And he knew that the foxy girl hated her big sister, though she hated the baby worse. Valentine knew their secrets — it was like collecting a family. They stayed with him, even though they'd left the room and were going down the stairs, and were crossing the hall. And he heard the front door close upon them, but he would always remember — it was as if they were his.

Part One
The Hills

One

Mama was always singing. She sat in her chair and sang about Eden of love and dawn's roseate hue. They were sacred songs: "Open Thou the crystal fountain ...", "Descend, O Holy Spirit, like a dove ... " In her songs there were silver moons and gates of pearl, but she was drab in her dusty black dress; her face looked smudged, like a pastel drawing you'd rubbed with a finger. It was to do with being sick, and though the label said it was the same tonic as taken in the Russian Imperial Family, it didn't do her any good.

But Mama was perfect with her fusty invalid smell, and the stain at her mouth from the teaspoons of tonic. And she took Syrup of Figs and the pink pills for pale people, but Dove didn't want her improved. She was always having to rest in her chair and she let Dove sit at her feet and lean against her knees. Her skirt spread about Dove like a cave and it was cosy, their love was special, and Mama told the story about the drive into the valley and coming to the angel and the lady in the house and how she'd wanted the new baby and how they drove away. Dove still had the corals that had been the old lady's present. And "Dove" wasn't just a name in a hymn, like "Rosa" and "Crystal". The dove on the stone angel's finger had protected Mama as she'd lain beneath it with the baby, who became Dove, inside her.

There was a cemetery in Appleton and Dove liked to wander there and read the names on the headstones and think about the people who'd died. The centre part, where the graves were of recent date, had paths planted with pine trees, and a latticed summer-house where ladies rested and gossiped over their watering-cans and baskets of flowers. But the old graves lay in a belt of scrub, wild and unkempt. Though their occupants were variously sleeping in Jesus, called home, or at rest, the grave's embrace didn't appear peaceful. Glass domes had been shattered so that the bouquets of china roses they sheltered were merely caged, now, by rusty spirals of wire. Marble angels had been felled by some un-known giant fist, and headstones flung down.

Granpa Nelson's grave was there and Dove had to fight her way, with fear of snakes at every turn, through tea-tree and thorn bush and a thicket of sharp-edged aloes to reach it. Waxy pellets of itchy powder spilled from leathery pods all about it. The tree they'd fallen from was hung with creamy bell flowers. The wind blew and the tree's stiff leaves rustled; the bell flowers bobbed and swayed with muted claps. Papery mauve and white everlastings poked up everywhere; there were trails of bull-ants, pellets of sheep dung. Dove couldn't imagine dying or growing old. She knew that her life would be extraordinary, for from the beginning she'd played a heroine's part.

But there was a crumple in the rose leaf. Dove remem-bered Papa and a shadow fell: he freckled her all over with gloom, he drew the virtue from her until she felt as if her soul would curl up. She didn't want a father, she didn't need him, and she hated him and he loved her — that was the worst thing.

Though she saw, of course, that he had no choice. For she was a prime favourite, as blithe as a lark, and won such good opinions from everyone about her. They couldn't help it as they admired her, and Papa couldn't either. She saw herself as he did: a little girl with her hair in long blonde curls like sticks of barley-sugar, very gentle and bright, rather pretty — and clever, too. She knew her weights and measures, and the dates of the kings and queens ... oh yes, she was a clever little monkey, for he failed to win the least affection from her but she hid her feelings splendidly.

His voice was swallowed by his beard; he was a cringing thing, so desperately in earnest and sincere. It was called being a New Man, and the change came after the return from Arden Valley. Mother and child had survived, and he gave thanks and went to the Tin Tabernacle, a place all silver shining among the gum trees. The Anglican church had a rose garden; the Methodist chapel still meant ladies wore cherries or ostrich tips on their hats. But at the Tabernacle they didn't bother with fashion, and gumnuts dropped on the tin roof. Bold boys looked in through the window, and saw them banging the pulpit with their harvesting hands, for they were Zealots of Christ with a campaign against bare arms and necks.

One day the boys saw Ebenezer Sparks in the seat for the penitent and heard him give his old self away. The wickedness went out of him and he stopped being tormented. He was forgiven, he forgave. From that day he was an abstainer who kept his black city clothes for Sunday — for everyday he dressed in moleskins, as he cleared and planted and put straight what had been neglected for years. He was someone strayed who'd returned to the flock. He was nothing. His spirit was gone.

Dove crouched, she hid from him. Under the bedclothes was a lovely warm place; she lay in her black secret nest and the world shrank small; she had blue veins in her cradling arms and her skin felt silky, milky pale; she fell into sleep breathing the starchy scent of her nightgown, feeling the tickle of baby ribbon at her throat. But he could even find her there. Sometimes at night candlelight surprised her — Papa held the candle and looked down on her. She lay still, pretending, until he crept away.

Each day began fresh, washed clean. She woke early and couldn't wait to explore. Past the kitchen door the world was new, with the seasons muddled, intermingled. Summer heat was already on the air, but the grass was wintry sleek with dew. The pigeons made their soft deep *boom-boom*, magpies warbled, little green parakeets hung upside down and nibbled at the Irish peach apples ... And now Dove was by the creek and the creek grass flowed out like hair. The lilies poked their tongues at the sky and she looked back and saw the house sink into the garden. The flowers were the colour of acid drops, and there were glistening bronze tints creeping everywhere, because the masquerading season was really autumn. It was her month, the month Dove was born, and it was the Hills where she belonged. They rose about her, tufted with the neat lines of orchards; they hid her, kept her safe. Yet each step she took made the landscape different. Now she looked up and saw the far off gum trees clustered; then, imperceptibly, they tapered away. Dove walked on, until the gums were lost behind fruit trees.

Crystal and Rosa didn't seem like Dove's sisters. They were so much older. Rosa was married to Will Priddle and Crystal came home for a holiday at Christmas, but mostly she lived in another person's house. Her black dresses were different to Mama's — they were smart, with swishing hems. It was funny to think that she was someone's housemaid.

Last time Crystal came home she had a velvet hat with Paris lace and violets. She gave Mama a box of French plums and she had seen the Governor, Lord Tennyson, and knew about dukes, duchesses, marquises, marchionesses, earls, countesses and all the lesser titles.

Will Priddle was a baker and the bakehouse kept being in different places. To begin with, Will had been the Appleton baker and Dove would see him with his floury hands and the smell of the new bread tickled her nostrils in a tantalizing manner. But after the wedding he and Rosa moved to the city. Now they lived on the Port Road and Rosa served in the shop and she'd started a penny library. There were books called *The Shears of Fate* and *Love's Mirage*.

Will was a little fellow with bow legs and a silly expression, but he was nice, very kind. Rosa was bossy and red in the face, but when they were only engaged and he came to see her in his Sunday suit, the red just looked like roses in the cheeks and she'd plucked away the hairs above her lip. For a while she was a big warm poppy of a girl, but now she had tempers and the hairs were so fierce that Dove thought of stinging nettles.

Rosa reckoned Will was soft and he always got cheated and they couldn't pay the rent. Something always went wrong. The new street that the bakery moved to was noisier and grubbier than the old one. Where they were now was near the gasometer.

Their son was called Ralph, and it seemed odd, but

Dove was his aunt. Before Ralph was born, Rosa wasn't allowed to eat anything, she could only drink barley water and orange juice. She went into hospital and had hot-water bottles all over her. It was a Friday night and she grunted and groaned through Saturday, until it was Sunday, but Ralph was a beautiful baby. They said it was the orange juice and barley water — his skin was like wax. Ralph had been born with a caul over his head: it meant he wouldn't drown. Rosa kept it wrapped in a hanky in her drawer. It looked awful, all yellowy.

Ralph had grown into a fat boy who had ill health. It was another thing that Rosa blamed Will for — she said it was the gas fumes that turned Ralph bilious. But when Dove came to visit she liked it. The traffic's din was pleasantly alarming, and she saw a Chinaman and found sixpence and there were little twisty streets — and if you trod on a crack you'd marry a black, if you stepped in a dog mess the smell lingered on your shoe all day.

But she wished she'd been there when it was the earthquake. For one night there started being rumbles and there'd been volcanic disasters at Martinique. "What, ho! She bumps," cried gentlemen and even gouty and rheumaticky ones showed the speed of athletes as they fled into the streets. Rosa said she'd never forget. It was a thrilling experience when the chairs danced and a curious throbbing ran up her legs.

Anything could happen in the city. In the Botanic Gardens the pine tree that was planted by the Duke of Clarence withered away simultaneously with the departure from life of that amiable young prince. When the Duke and Duchess of Cornwall came, two thousand pigeons soared into the sky and at night there were fireworks. Caskets of stars rushed towards the Milky Way;

44

there were storms of golden snow and portraits of the royal visitors traced in fire against a background of inky blackness.

Nothing much happened in the Hills. The storekeeper went out shooting rabbits and shot a fox as well — it was the first sighted in the district, and he had it hanging in the shop verandah as a novelty for several days. Old Mrs Cook who kept cows was chopping wood, and a piece of wattle wood flew up and knocked her eye out. The publican's wife had twins and one was named Emma Maria, the other Maria Emma, and they were very much alike.

The South African War was over and people had stopped singing "Soldiers of the Queen" and "Sons of the Sea". For a time men were heroes and Dove gave the money she got out of the Christmas pudding to the Patriotic Fund. But the year Queen Victoria died the War ended. It was strange having a king. Travice Thorn had collected twenty-five empty Cameo cigarette packets. It meant he'd get a coronation souvenir. He could choose from a portrait of The King, The Queen, Lord Roberts and Lord Kitchener.

Mrs Thorn had named her younger son after the hero of a book she had read. Travice and Dove were so often together that it seemed they were brother and sister.

The Thorns lived up the road from the Sparkses in a white house with bright coloured geraniums on the verandah. Dove liked running under the row of stately sugar gums that cast such a grateful shade on the pathway in summer.

Mrs Thorn was a charming woman, artistic, with fine expressive eyes. She had painted the picture of the knight in armour and the maiden dressed in flowing robes on the folding screen; she shut her eyes and swayed in a ladylike manner when she played the piano. She had the most elegant drawing-room in Appleton. It was a pleasure to sit on her sofa and admire the needlepoint cushions and the wallpaper with its pattern of cabbage roses, and listen to her talk of the characters in the novels she'd read as if they were her friends. There was a lady who didn't know it was indecent to wear diamonds before the gas was lit, and a gentleman like Captain Moonlight who was a bit of a dandy, besides being a bushranger, and wore gold tassels to his boots.

Mrs Thorn had grown up in a grand house with servants and couldn't get used to doing her own housework. She was always saying that she was lucky to have a practical daughter. Issy Thorn was the sort of girl who would never get married. If she'd dressed up as a man you would have called her handsome. Because she wore skirts her gruff voice and Roman emperor's profile seemed absurd.

Her brother George's moustache hid a hare-lip. Whenever Dove came near him she wrinkled her nose. George's strong body smelled fusty. It wasn't just sweat — mixed with the straightforward sweaty smell was the queer scent of something else, perhaps the scent of stale excitement or fright. George was so shy of anyone female — even a child like Dove — that he made her feel uncomfortable. He never looked at her when he talked; he kept shifting from one foot to the other as if he were nervous. But George was a hard worker and ambitious. He kept on at his father to buy more land. He said they should go into wheat.

Issy and George were their father's children. Mr Thorn was big and quiet, too. At ease, outdoors, going about his everyday tasks, he turned awkward when he entered the house. Like Issy and George he seemed intimidated by Mrs Thorn. Yet he was proud of her; he was always bringing her presents from town.

Travice was the apple of his mother's eye. He was the queerest looking fellow you could fancy. His body seemed all arms and legs; there was usually an inch or two of wrist and sock visible at the end of his sleeves and trousers. His sandy hair refused to make any parting; his nose looked dabbed on as an afterthought. But he had a pleasing smile. When he grinned it was a sight to see: the smile spread over his face, until Dove felt that his whole body must be grinning and glowing with happiness. He was always in trouble, always in mischief. He was the one who brought the paper bag of singing locusts to school, and put the three fat grubs in Teacher's desk.

Mr Thorn kept pigs. This one was a porker, that one a light baconer. Snowflake, the Yorkshire sow, was as pretty as paint. Flirt, the natty Berkshire, was a magnificent creature, long and roomy, with a fine covering of hair.

Usually Mr Thorn was mild; when he killed the pig he was different. He was a stranger as he shot it in the forehead and lifted it into the wheelbarrow and put it on the table under the pepper tree. Then he made a gash across its throat and Granny Thorn was there to catch the blood in her little bowl to make black pudding. They poured boiling water from the copper over the pig and scraped off its bristles with saucepan lids. After they cut it up the meat hung from the tree in a calico bag until it was pickled in brine.

Once Granny had lived in a villa surrounded by a fig garden on the top of Appleton Hill. After she was widowed and grew old she came to live in her son's apple house. It was a little low-down place of wattle sticks and mud, where the apples used to be stored. When Granny came, Mr Thorn put in a chimney and raised the floor. It was comfortable inside with china dogs on the mantelpiece, and Granny papered her walls afresh each spring. She used flour and water paste and the newspaper's pages. Up on Granny's walls was the serial story and the ad. for Bon Ton corsets and the hints for garden and greenhouse.

Granny Thorn was a lady of a bygone era, picturesque to a degree, with her old-fashioned bonnet and shawl. After evening service at church she shook hands with Granpa Priddle, because he was the oldest male, and she was the oldest female attendant, and they never knew whether there would be another Sunday for either.

Sometimes a Presbyterian minister visited Appleton and the doors of the disused kirk stood open and the Psalms of David, metrical version, rose upon the air. Then it was Scotch Sunday, but Roman Sunday occurred more regularly, for every third week a priest came to serve his scattered flock. That Sunday there was a long string of vehicles on the Appleton Road and Dove saw Callaghans and Donohues and Caffreys ... And the Tin Tabernacle didn't count ... And the Methodists were once divided into Wesleyan and Primitive, Bible Christian and New Connexion, but amalgamation made them one and the chapel was ugly and Dove disliked going with Mama — she wished she were Church of England like Travice and could see the stained glass and kneel on the embroidered cushion and attend the Easter Festival.

And Christ had risen, so nine plum puddings boiled merrily in the vicarage copper and Granny Thorn made one, too, and it was a monster, the largest seen in the district. And after coconut shies, Aunt Sally, and other games of skill, dinner was served in a large marquee.

The archdeacon knocked on the table with his knife handle for grace, and then everyone set to work in earnest. What appetites some of them had. They worked through plates heaped up with sucking pig, turkey and goose, to plum pudding, apple pie and jam tarts — then some were known to start all over again. It was customary to eat blancmange with your pudding. The smoking heat of the one, and the smooth cold of the other, made pleasant contrast.

But the Methodists had a picnic to the waterfalls where there was a pool of unfathomable depth and the water was of such icy quality as to produce gooseflesh on the casual bather.

It wasn't the city, but there was always something to do. On winter evenings there were sixpenny entertainments in the schoolroom, and once the tableau was "Rock of Ages" and the postmistress was wonderful, draped in butter-muslin, clasping the cross. And Appleton was a great place for blackberries — parties went out with their billycans in season. And there were drifts of snowdrops, and coral fern in the creek.

TWO

It seemed things could never change. Dove's life in Appleton would always stay the same, with Mama taking her medicine and resting and Papa effecting numerous improvements to his fruit garden. And he had Rome Beauty, Cleopatra and the Irish peach apples and Winter Duchess and Josephine pears; and his orchard was rendered rabbit proof, but there was always golden gorse to eradicate, and the starlings, the rosellas, the silver-eyes could be credited with damaged fruit.

It was home and the blue sky soared high and a gallah kept flying until it was tiny, just a bright pink feather. The wattle's hard pimples burst into velvety fluff dots like the spots on the new Paris veilings. Bees scrambled in the purple bell flowers and even the magpies were marauders, but they destroyed the codlin moth. Some of Papa's apples were going off to England — in the fruit garden he was enterprising, but he was a scarecrow with his straggly beard and he was as old and twisted as the apple tree that leaned on the house, the mulberry tree by the gate. Those trees would always be there, for they were part of the pattern that meant home. The Hills sheltered numerous little towns, but Dove knew only Appleton, it was all she wanted.

At the Diamond Jubilee a concert had been got up to

procure an invalid chair for the district, to be lent out to the sick and afflicted. And Granny Thorn stopped walking and wallpapering and she didn't hold her bowl to catch the pig's blood, so there was no more black pudding; and Granny used to sing to the accompaniment of her sister's guitar and she nearly married the man from Melbourne. But she was young then, and now she was old, and she started riding in the Diamond Jubilee chair, and at the Jubilee concert the three Miss Almonds had sung "We'll all go a-hunting today". The youngest had a shining rope of black hair down her back and her eyes were grey with long lashes. She was the Miss Almond who drove about with the dearest pair of ponies imaginable. Their little hoofs scampered along, and people always knew when they were coming, their sound was different from the other sounds of horses on the road. She was nearly overcome with giggles at the concert, but sang bravely to the end, and then people couldn't believe it, but she caught consumption and died. And the apple house stopped being a model of neatness, its door stood open and no one cared, for Granny Thorn died, too.

But Granpa Priddle was left — Dove prayed he'd stay for ever. He wore a black skull-cap because of the cold and had a clear-cut picture of primitive times. But death got him, as well; the generations were scattered, and they chopped down the pines in the cemetery because nothing would grow beneath them and rose bushes were planted in their stead. They flourished exceedingly and there was a clean-up in the old part: it was no longer wild and snaky. It was God's rose-planted acre, but Dove didn't go there any more.

For suddenly death was real. Granpa Nelson had been a man, also; he'd walked about and laughed and tended the vine at the back of the house, and then his body went into the earth. And a Sparks could die, too — Papa would (Dove wouldn't care much) and Mama (it would be unbearable) and (it was unthinkable) even Dove.

People vanished, and their dwelling-places, too. A cottage once stood halfway up Appleton Hill. Now it had gone, but the briar that grew in its garden was its memento all over a paddock.

But, thinking back, it seemed that Miss Almond had been fated to die. For she was too pretty and fascinating to live long and though her decline had been pitiable, her death was romantic: there were flower smells all about her when she lay in her coffin and she was thinner, yes, but the lilies and roses pressed close, the expression on her face was agreeable. She was the Sleeping Beauty, and they'd combed out her hair — she seemed to sleep in a bower of silky tresses. Her sisters sobbed convulsively, but no tears flowed (she'd been so pretty she quite left them in the shade). At the next sixpenny concert their duet was ''The Wind and the Harp'' … And Granny had been old — it was a blessing she was taken, and the Thorns had more money, now, their drawing-room was nicer than ever. The new things were twin whatnots and a picture of the Bridge of Sighs. For a while Granny's china dogs stood on the mantel, but Mrs Thorn thought them old-fashioned and sent them, with the engraving of the Christians being eaten by the Colosseum lions, to the Church of England bazaar. Time passed, and Granny's dying didn't seem too bad and Granpa Priddle had been an embarrass-ment. He wouldn't stay in and read his Bible but hobbled about on two sticks and had a way of turning up at various houses at meal times, much to the distress of his daughters who were most respectable, and liked him to keep at home.

Dove stopped worrying, and went back to feeling that it couldn't happen to her. And it would be ages before Mama succumbed, though she sang about dying every day. In Mama's songs, in any case, dying took you home. It would be the happiest day of your life, when you entered into the perpetual worship of Paradise.

So Dove concentrated on living and went on some lovely rambling scrambling walks with Travice. They walked miles and paddled in creeks and found hyacinth orchids and greenhoods. One day they rambled so far that the Hills became foreign. The Appleton apples were picked, but here they still hung on the trees. Evening fell, the sun went in, and the country was cleft with shadows. Dove felt scared, but soon they saw the glimmering lights of home. By the big mulberry tree she let Travice kiss her.

But a girl shouldn't like it when glittering pig blood flowed, and to walk with Travice would make her a subject of remark. So Dove sowed sweet peas and watered the garden and Mama taught her tatting. But she wanted to run barefoot and bathe in the creek. Travice had been like her brother, she missed him.

Suddenly Mrs Thorn was a stranger. She was Mama's dearest friend, but she stopped coming to visit. When she saw Dove she smiled coldly, her eyes were malicious. She loved Travice jealously, he was her favourite possession, though he had an awkward body and jug-handle ears.

He was different from the other boys. He didn't shoot at the rosella parrots or join the band that went out hunting the nocturnal possum. But he wasn't wishy-washy. He liked football and was a persevering and promising scholar when he wasn't playing tricks. He was always getting into scrapes. Miss Donahue had a black and white cow and Travice whitewashed it, and she took the strange beast to the pound. Yet he was kind-hearted to a fault ... his very affection seemed to bring trouble with it. Mrs Thorn disliked Dove now. And when Travice had the pet magpie it died, because his hands were so much less tender than his heart. If he was lent anything, he lost it. If he was given anything, he broke or spoiled it.

For years Dove's day had been patterned by the school bell. In the morning its sound was chiding: "Hurry, hurry," it urged and there was no more meandering, no time to pick the bunch of shivery grass or hunt the trap-door spider's home. Instead, she must speed to salute the flag, to tiptoe march away from freedom. Outside the day went on, but Dove couldn't see it. She was imprisoned in a room where the windows were high up to prevent the scholars peeping out. There was a stale smell of chalk dust and pencils. The old Queen looked down in her crown and garter ribbon; the blowflies danced at the pane. Orchards and tickling wattle blossom were exchanged for pussy-tails in a pickle jar stuck with shells, a miniature wheat field sprouting from cotton-wool. Though school was bearable if it was Composition; even Mental Arithmetic wasn't too bad. If she got the sum right Teacher would toss the tiny sea-shell for her to catch at. And when it was her birthday she rode on the dappled rocking-horse, and when they sang "Ye banks and braes" the hair ribbons and sashes were pink or blue, denoting soprano and alto distinctions. But those were early infant days. The years went by like magic. It was as if a spell had fallen upon the schoolroom. Only the Queen was different — Alexandra smiled on them, now, flaunting her swan's neck, her pearls. But everything else was the same: smells and flies, pickle jars and wheat field. The oilcloth map of the world hung before the blackboard on its cord, the Empire coloured in blush pink. Teacher's stick made its steady *peck-peck* as it advanced on the capitals of Europe. She stood there, petrified by time, pince-nez slipping down her nose, moo-cow voice droning on ... thick ankles, plum-coloured dress scurfy on the shoulders. But the Fifth Class had been hustled on to childhood's outskirts. Once the Certificate exam was sat for, school had no more use of them: a day was coming when its bell would toll Dove away for ever. And now, an ending in sight, an escape route guaranteed, Dove forgot the punishments, the horror of decimal points, the words she couldn't spell. She could only think nostalgically of the good times. The concert where they sang "The Firefly" in golden gauze and silver tissue and butter-muslin wings. Hide-and-seek and skipping, hoppy and chasey and knucklebones at recess. And one-two-three-four-five-six-seven:

> All good men must go to Heaven,
> Penny on the water, twopence on the sea,
> Threepence on the railway,
> Out goes SHE.

It was strange to stay home every day. Dove swept the verandah and her broom made a sad sound and big white clouds moved across the sky. It was summer and Mama's walk was bobbing, bent over, as she walked between the strawberry bed's rows, searching for ripe juicy fruit. Flat wild roses bloomed everywhere, their petals like the saucers of a doll's tea-set; the leaves of the agapanthus resembled glistening green liquorice straps. The pigeons' *coo-roo* was a constant complaining rumble; the guinea fowls had strange swollen bodies, patterned like chain-mail, and their cowled heads, blotched with white, were sinister. But the baby ducklings wobbled fuzzily on rubbery black feet, the bantam chicks had beaks like sea-shells. Each day it grew hotter. Flap-winged butterflies wavered crazily on the air; the dusty hillsides were pelted with a flickering lace of bleached grass. Summer's colours were muted: beige, pale lilac, pink — the colours of summer puddings: Floating Island, Convent Cream, Narcissus Blancmange.

At Christmas, Crystal came home from the city. It was a come-down for her to return to Appleton because she was used to a mansion with rooms full of gilded cabinets upon which stood statuettes from the antique in bronze. In Appleton, talking to the butcher and the grocer, Crystal seemed a grand lady. She had an elegant walking costume and a shot silk sunshade and a swan-like manner of holding herself. But her lips were thin and her hair was red, and her affectations and airs were tiresome. Crystal hardly spoke to Mama; Papa was below her notice. She lay on the couch and ate clove drops and wished she were back at the mansion.

Now and then Crystal confided. Her face stayed still, but her nostrils went like little quivering animals as her thin mouth talked on and on. Her eyes looked through Dove, as if she weren't there, and she told of how she was going to London. Crystal's eyes were dreamy, yet intent; her voice was fierce and sure. The Hotel Cecil was a good address ... London was where Lord Wemyss was, and the Trocadero had old-gold walls. In the crypt of St Paul's you were among the dead heroes. Crystal would meet men with fair-skinned shoulders.

The couch she lay on was old and battered; and in the next room Mama sang about the night of doubt and sorrow; and through the window Dove could see the path to the lavatory. It was lined with Ophelia roses, but it led on to that dangling fly-paper, that smell ... but Crystal talked marvellously and the hazy summer sky behind the pane turned midnight black, for *there* it was winter and snow fell like castor-sugar from the dredger. London was a land of mystery and latest hats, and in Regent Street myriads scrurried. Every one of them was a stranger, but Crystal would be bold enough to brave them, by way of a P&O steamer.

But sometimes when she talked her voice wasn't confiding, confidential. She talked flatly, as if she didn't care who heard. She was someone defeated as she complained that she couldn't stand it much longer. For she was scrabbling, hurrying over everything, and yet everything had to be perfect. It didn't sound like a mansion any more — just Josephine Villa, somewhere off the Beach Road. And Crystal had to get his breakfast — it was always bread and milk for the master and he was an old man like a child, but fussy. She had to cut his bread into squares, and it mustn't be crumbly, and all the squares had to be the same size. He was a dribbly old man with a bib and a newspaper tablecloth. Crystal would go mad, even though the pay was good. She had to empty his chamber-pot when she was meant for a life across the sea in the same world as Miss Alice de Rothschild.

●●●

Everything changed. To begin with, the Thorns left Appleton. They sold the house and the orchard and the pigs, and all Mrs Thorn's drawing-room elegancies went off on a trolley pulled by two horses. George's championing of agriculture had finally had effect: people said Mr Thorn had turned ambitious, too, and thought Appleton wasn't big enough. The cause might also have been that Travice sent Dove a picture postcard of the Misses Phyllis and Zena Dare. They were actresses, but the worst thing was that he wrote on the card "with love". Mama made Dove send it back and Mrs Thorn found out and not long afterwards the Thorns sold at a profit and went to live in the Mallee.

It sounded like a foreign place to Dove — another country, but they only called it that because of the trees. Those little scrubby mallee trees grew everywhere and the soil was light and sandy: it was a land of promise, ideal for wheat-growing, a hundred miles to the east. Previously it had been held by the squatters, but now the Government had surveyed it and there was a land boom. People from all walks of life were taking up sections.

Then Mama went, too. It was a night the same as any other. Papa sat at the table writing in his book. It had a leather cover and marbled end-papers, and every year had its page with an entry for each month telling things like when he'd planted the onions and cleared the stinkweed; grubbed the blackberries and sprinkled bonedust. And there was a part where he wrote in the recipe for tanning skins and the cures for diphtheria and seminal weakness, but this night he was adding to his list of the different fruit trees. He'd done pears and apples and apricots on other nights; now, he was starting on the cherries. Their names were stirring: Belle de Orleans, that was tender and juicy; Heart of Midlothian, that could be medium deep red or fine-flavoured black ... Ohio Beauty, Waterloo ... Dove sat on the hearthrug and leaned against Mama's legs and it was cold that night, they had a fire. There was a spicy smell from the burning blue gum and Mama's knitting needles had stopped clicking. Dove was half asleep. Lazily, from a long way off, she heard the scratch of Papa's pen and the spitting sound as sparks flew. She was too near the fire but she didn't care, not even if she paid for the luxury later with a red nose. Outside, the wind made a sobbing sound, but somehow a stillness overlay everything. Mama sat so quiet.

A rose bush grew on her grave, there were always flowers in a vase, and behind the headstone Dove kept the polishing rags. As she rubbed the cold marble she had a feeling — oh, if she could only get down into the earth she would find Mama. Her songs had always been about a world above — up there were pearly gates, harps of gold — but Dove wanted to sink below the dust, the crust of leaves. She would never smile again, or look in the mirror, for flesh didn't last.

After Mama died, Papa was no longer the New Man. He went back to being someone Dove had never known. His nightly wrestlings with the Spirit were loud enough to be audible to passers-by on the road outside. He was tormented, tortured and she shrank from him but he didn't notice. He was alone in a private place and the grass grew high, the garden became a wilderness that pressed against the house. He would live for ever, and this would be Dove's life: tending someone she hated and she couldn't bear it.

•••

He was mad and Dove was afraid of him and her anger hid deep inside her. He took the picture of Mama framed in velvet from the mantelpiece and cradled it in his hands. He was out in all weathers and when he came into the house he didn't see Dove, but Mama seemed to be with him all the time. He was more like a tree or a bush than a man. The birds threw their hard notes at him, the wind knotted his beard, the rain stained and whipped him.

Ebenezer Sparks had prayed and pleaded — at last God sent His answer. When the storm came Dove cowered in bed, but Papa answered the knock of the thunder, he ran to welcome the violet night sky and the furnace of flames. The stars blazed and crackled, there was a fire in the sky. The earth heaved and split; the mulberry tree reared; the apple trees waved skinny fingers. Ebenezer climbed into the sky and blundered among stars and winds and the moon, the sun. He felt the years go past him; he heard the ticking of time. He was back with Daisy in the orchard. Petals fluttered, she was full of little secret ways, but now his body swayed towards the wilderness. Cockatoos and gallahs screech-ed in the gum trees. He was a ghost, a dying man, but it was the adventure when he tramped on for ever. Trees assumed fantastic shapes, there were merciless suns. The kangaroos were black, of great size and strength; there were masses of sharp-edged rocks, the hills were wild and tangled. It was a country so terribly stony but suddenly it was the Garden of Eden. Saltbush and blue-bush came alive, there were little feathery leaves and the desert was a sleeping paradise, the sunburned stones of the stark gibber plains were hidden by green carpets of verdure. The grass waved and lapped him. There was no more despair but only bright hope and their lashes came down but they couldn't tame him. The scars slipped off his back — he was young, fresh-skinned, again. He was as strong as an angel and he heard the prayers of the saints. He saw the bloody moon and the white horse, the red horse, the black horse, the pale horse. And his name was Death.

Boughs creaked, birds flapped, the stars swam in hot circles. Papa was under the earth, he was up in the sky. There was a roar of thunder, and lightning swept up the mulberry tree; roots tore and snapped, the tree fell down. A pane of glass in the parlour doorway smashed and Dove thought it was the end of the world.

Three

For a while Dove wore mourning and it was a pity, people said — she'd been plucked from a cottage with vine tracery across the verandah to live near the gasometer and the foundry. How sad it was, they sighed — the ladies who came to the bakery to buy milk loaf and subscribe to the penny library. They shook their heads and Rosa masked the snap in her eyes. So sad, she agreed, but his death to her meant merely money. Rosa's papa had died years ago. Just once at the funeral she looked at Dove straight. For an instant, over the St Joseph lilies, her smile was a snarl and: *You did it,* said her gunpowdery eyes. Suddenly Rosa surprised Dove, she was terrible in black. *I knew him different,* her hating eyes said. *You changed him,* she said to Dove.

Then Rosa hid her eyes in a hanky and was just a matron, sulky-mouthed, clutching Will Priddle's arm — though he was a baker she scorned, floury-fingered, bow-legged, and sometimes there was string in the bread. Will wasn't high class; he did milk and pipe and sandwich loaf. He made penny rolls and buns, too (once someone found a cigarette butt instead of a currant, but Will didn't care). He stayed a man from the Hills. All the Appleton Priddles had his face, and Dove liked to be near him. Because of Will, the Port Road didn't seem such a foreign place.

But Rosa had never felt at home there. She disliked the gas smell, the soap factory smell, the bottle-ohs and dustmen that did for neighbours. It was rumoured that down the side streets were Chinamen with backyards full of poppies who did torture, drove wedges of green bamboo under fingernails. There were glass jags along the top of the wall, and the Gaol was nearby. It was morbid, melancholy — when there was a hanging you heard the death bell toll.

The bakery horse was called Tiny. He cut his throat on the galvanized iron fence and they found him dead in the yard. So Papa's demise was timely. For the Appleton house and the Cleopatras, the Rome Beauties, the snug gullies of peach trees, the lilies by the creek, the wattle blossom that was like solidified sunshine had been sold, and the grand total divided into three. Crystal sailed off to London with her share; Dove must wait to come of age to inherit; Rosa said "We will buy a new house, a new horse."

And they rented another bakehouse and this time it wasn't joined on to where they lived. In the new street a bank manager dwelt opposite and there were bay windows, lead lights, Marseilles tiles; Shirley poppies, Crimson Rambler, pansy borders. But Rosa's little girl ruined it. She was plain and had headaches; she was so thin that Rosa felt ashamed she should be seen out of doors. So Peggy Priddle sat on a chair at the window and looked past the flywire and across the slippery red verandah. In the new suburb fences were replaced by hedges: pittosporum, cypress, carob, olive, and privet that was a splendid bee plant. They were hedges without thorns, and beyond them Peggy never saw anyone strange; passers-by were mostly other ladies who might have been Rosa. They were just as proper as she was, handsome women in their prime, who walked and dressed in a similar way. Bent forward, their bodices bobbing and swaying, they swept down the street in their Amazonian cloth dresses in shades of wine, reseda, bottle-green.

Rosa had come alive again, she had hope among the blood-red brick bungalows. And there were orange-tiled roofs, art metal ceilings and Rosa had an imitation marble eight-day clock, a bamboo hall-stand, a folding armchair in polished walnut. Will said it was madness, but she kept buying. The bedroom was wonderful with its fumed oak suite in the Egyptian style; and there was a cut glass hairpin box, an electroplated hairbrush, and the Parisian bedstead in black and brass rose up — high-backed, massive, with hand-polished pillars.

At night Rosa took off her combinations and the corset that left the cruel red marks. Oh, she was dented, stamped all over, and her big breasts swung loose, they were pear-shaped (Glou Morceau, Josephine — Papa used to grow them). But then she heard Will Priddle coming up the passage ... he only saw a lady in a nainsook nightie — plaiting her hair; folding back the honeycomb quilt; climbing between the calm cold sheets.

But Rosa had Ralph. He was a fat boy and on bath night she washed his back. The geyser snorted and Ralph was modest, he covered his privates with the flannel. Rosa rubbed with Pears' soap until his skin gleamed pink (but he had a weak heart, he took aconite pills for fevers). Dove didn't like Ralph. His piggy eyes were shrewd, he had a funny way of looking at girls.

Dove was no one, now; her opinion didn't count. In summer, dressed in white, she was pale as a ghost and the smart suburb pressed against her like a bandage. She knew she would never escape. Who'd imagine she'd ever been a heroine who'd been snatched at by a rich old lady? She still had the corals that had been Mrs Arden's present, but it seemed they were nothing to do with her. The days merged into weeks that were alike. Dove dusted and polished and went to the shops; she shared a bed with Peggy and on Sunday there was church. The Sunday School picnic was a treat to look forward to, and when the great day came the sea was taunting, but no one fell off the jetty; though it was fun when the children made huge castles of sand, one for the girls and one for the boys. Then they were told to run away while the teacher stuffed the castles with oranges. The children were called back and the sandcastles were rapidly demolished.

Once Dove had been as happy as the Sunday School children. She'd been sure there was treasure, and she had Travice for a friend. They were so affectionate that there were prospects of the childish romance developing into a more serious attachment. But presently their ways lay apart, and it was sad. Dove cried as she lay in bed beside Peggy and listened to the dull grinding of her teeth, which was one of the symptoms of worms, the children's enemy.

Dove started taking long walks. She walked until the new suburb petered out and its place was taken by a rag-tag gipsy land of dairies and poultry farms and lucerne paddocks. Once she saw the cross-country hunt. There were horses and men in red coats. She heard the dogs baying, and watched them jump over the briar fences. And there were boxthorn hedges with their bright berries that tasted like tomatoes; tall Kaffir apple trees with their golden fruit. One day she came to the part that was the paradise for feathered friends. In the distance was the stately home covered in ivy where the old captain who was the bird lover lived. He took captive any boys he caught harming birds and shut them in a room until just before dark. Magpies strutted on his verandahs; peacocks perched on his balconies; pheasants, curlews and mopokes roamed at will. People always knew when bad weather approached, because the peacocks never failed to screech a warning.

There were reeds about Dove, now, and she had come to a river bordered with willows and giant gums. Somewhere across its further bank was the soldier boy. At sunset he practised his bugle. It was evening, but the chords of Reveille sounded eerily over the paddocks.

It was 1910 and Crystal wrote regularly from London, where the Suffragetes were degrading womanhood by throwing stones and Miss Lily Elsie went roller-skating at Olympia in her Merry Widow hat. And Crystal knew, too, about the chanticleer craze in hats with the head of the bird on the brim, and the rage for mummy skirts in lapis-lazuli blue. And in Paris the Seine overflowed, and Mount Etna erupted, and His Majesty was taking his usual recuperative course at Biarritz.

But in May the King died and people were magically transformed from wearers of gay spring toilettes into mourners garbed in the sable trappings of deepest woe.

Crystal saw the funeral. A noble gathering of kings and princes followed the bier; next came the military figures; then the wee beastie, a white-haired Irish terrier, the late King's favourite dog, being led by a kilted Scotch gillie. All those who had houses along the funeral route rented their windows at exorbitant prices, and men sold boxes to stand on and charged double for the official programme. But the worst thing was the crowd who tore the laurel wreaths which were hung along the Green and Hyde Park railings to pieces and sold bunches of leaves at a shilling.

Mourning was the pose of the hour, and sweet and cake shop displays were charming. The shop windows were decorated with Czar violets; every cake was sugared with violet icing and sweets were only shown in mauve colour, their boxes tied with royal purple ribbon. So far was the mourning habit carried, that fashionable women sent their white poodles, King Charles spaniels and brown Pomeranians to the country, and substituted black dogs of every description.

But in Kensington Gardens and Hyde Park the hawthorns were flowering thickly like great shower bouquets of pink and white. The tall chestnuts, too, were covered in blossom; while the brilliant yellow laburnums and copper beeches were doing their best to add to the glory of everything. The grass was vividly green, the flower beds blazed with colour. When the band played in the afternoon and the horses began to throng the Park, there was no more cheerful or interesting spot in all London.

Suddenly Crystal's letters were different. It was as if she'd forgotten King Edward completely. She no longer mourned; she didn't even give King George or Queen Mary a mention. Her letters were about fashion and the mysterious Mr Gerard. "Crystal was always a dreamer," said Rosa, raising her eyebrows. "She'll soon be in a pickle if she doesn't come down to earth." Rosa reckoned that if Crystal wasn't still a lady's maid, she was one of those nurses pushing a perambulator in the Gardens, and it was probably where she'd let him pick her up. Crystal had always been a liar. Mr Gerard ("my dear Robbie" she called him, if you please) was a gentleman who sounded too good to be true.

The letters got better and better. Crystal wrote about Melba as the hapless Mimi in *La Boheme* and Ranelagh, the famous club and grounds of English polo. And Florence Nightingale died and Mrs Crippen's remains were discovered in the cellar at Hilldrop Crescent. And dear Robbie had bought Crystal the sweetest evening frock in Rickett's blue satin. Rosa said its dishabille was a disgrace — it had about as much warmth in it as would keep a canary bird alive. Then she sneered worse because the next letter told that they were married. He might be a second Dr Hawley Harvey Crippen — he might be anyone. She was a fool, said Rosa; but "I am so happy" she wrote. They honeymooned in Spain, and Crystal was even in the know there. Who'd imagine that when the Spanish Queen attended a bullfight, an ordeal she loathed, she avoided offending the feelings of her people, and saved her own feelings as well, by the simple expedient of having milk-white lenses put in her field-glasses.

Now and then she wrote from the Maida Vale address, but she didn't say much about Mr Gerard. Only that there was something very wholesome and British about him, that he was from the ranks of the noblest and oldest families. He took her to the stately ballrooms of Belgravia and for a holiday to Italy, that Wellington boot shaped land. Venice was built on a hundred islands, the principal industries of Florence were straw-plaiting and silkworms, Rome had the dome of St Peter's ... she might have been cribbing from the geography book — Italy was as unreal as Mr Gerard. Then her letters stopped coming and Dove began to forget her.

London was a dreamland where ladies wore ninon

blouses, even when it snowed, and whizzed along in a tube beneath the pavement, and dyed their hair tomato shade with henna. For a while the great city had been real — the place where Dove's sister walked about, a place she might even aspire to visit. In London you could get pink violets, green carnations, blue roses and anything might have happened to Crystal, for her letters had ceased coming, but Rosa merely shrugged.

She had disappeared like Mama and Papa and Travice before her, but Rosa said not to worry. If there'd been an accident, or worse, they would have been notified and, in any case, Rosa had worries of her own. There was Ralph's heart, and Peggy was still skeleton skinny, and the bakery was losing trade. There were fashions in bread as well as in clothes. In the smart suburb, ladies with satin revers demanded Vienna and French loaf for their afternoon teas, but Will kept baking pipe and milk and sandwich loaves even though it was a new age with telephones and electric trams, and "aviation" was the fashionable word. M de Lesseps had flown across the English Channel, and afternoon tea fancies would have been a good seller, but Will didn't have initiative, he wouldn't do iced whirls or chocolate Venetians. He stayed countrified, uncouth. He wasn't averse to a game of two-up or Yankee grab; his favourite habitat was the old Sir John Barleycorn where the barmaids were pets. Rosa couldn't bear Will Priddle near her; she had become a lady who lived for her church. Sunday was horrid. Dove felt its gloom as soon as she awoke. The day had an empty feeling, because she wasn't allowed to do anything — everything interesting was considered work. She had to clean her shoes the night before, and dinner was Saturday's left-overs, and it seemed she was constantly setting off for church with a threepenny bit for collection tucked inside her glove.

But it was a friend of Rosa's from church who was a member of the Wattle League, and arranged for Dove to be one of the young ladies who sold sprays of the national flower on Wattle Day.

For in the city, on a day in spring, there were flashes of yellow in buttonholes, and shop windows were artistically decked and statues were wreathed. It had been decided that the wattle blossom stood for home and country, for the purity of its domestic life, for the generosity of Nature, for the brightness and colour of its sun-flooded fields, and for the nobler emotions of its people. It seemed that the beauty and fragrance of the country had been brought into the town. Trains from the Hills steamed in, festooned with wattle from end to end; street vehicles of all kinds, from the coster's cart and the corporation trolley, to the most stylish brougham and the finest motor car, were decorated. Companies of ladies visited the hospitals and charitable institutions, distributing largesse of spring's golden harvest.

Dove wore her best white dress and her hat was daintily trimmed. She knew she looked nice; she blushed becomingly as gentlemen stopped at her tray. It hung suspended from her shoulders by satin ribbons; the sprigs of wattle it held were so bright and cheerful, their sneezy scent tickled her nose ... and suddenly she saw a tall young man with a wattle spray in his buttonhole already. His face was tanned, he was staring at her as a gentleman never should. But she didn't mind, she wasn't little Miss Sparks now — demure and dutiful, gentle and dependent; instead, she was a stranger — someone sparkling, who bubbled over with energy and good spirits. The young man's eyes were frank and merry, his nose was ridiculous, and Dove's heart began to beat in an uneasy way. "Don't you know me?" Travice Thorn asked. Had she forgotten the walks they used to take? Didn't she remember the pigs?

Four

Her hands trembled when she opened his letters and it didn't matter what he'd written, Dove's mind said the secret words for him. She'd thought about their chance Wattle Day encounter so often that reality's sharp edges had conveniently faded away. Remembering him truly, her mind saw merely a blur; but, dreaming, Dove knew him exactly. He was a strong brave man of the bush, he was the boy she used to have mulberry fights with — she could turn him into anyone she pleased. Whoever he was, their correspondence was romantic — it had to be, for, please God, life didn't just mean you'd end up like Will and Rosa with one voice nagging on, nutmeg-grater raw, and the other answering back so dull and defeated, then suddenly exploding, saying words that were a sin. Rosa and Will were a warning, for you knew their lives were over though they would stay alive for years and years yet. The freshness of their beginnings had been smothered away under a load of necessities for civilized living — electroplated marmalade jar, nickel-capped bamboo pot-stand, cut glass decanters, damask table-cloths ...

Then the letter came that invited Dove to holiday with the Thorns, and because of it there was a journey that seemed as if it would go on for ever. There were some stiff grades to negotiate and at each of the sidings there was a little gathering of settlers, and long halts were necessary to disgorge innumerable packages from the goods vans. But at last it was Dove's turn to make that hazardous jump from footboard to ground. Travice was there to meet her with the buggy. There were forty more miles to the farm.

He was nothing like the person he was mostly meant to be — the hero she'd written most of the letters to — but she didn't mind. His face was tanned, he was tall, but you could never call him handsome. He wasn't as bad as the child he'd been, but he still had that nose. Though his ears were improved and his body was a better fit for his clothes.

Straight away they were comfortable together, they talked without cease all the way. Travice made her see the land differently. From the train window it had been too subtle for her. She'd longed for parrot colours — not pale creams and duns, fawns and ochres; not those huddled bushes and spindly trees, that bleached sweep of sky. Sitting beside him in the buggy it seemed another country. The trees were tipped with rubbery red leaves, the grass was blue-grey; there were white stones, pinky earth. The neat bushes drew together, the land was so gentle. Dust flew and fanned about them as they drove down the rough limestone road. Every so often they were confronted by a sand-hill: they bumped up over it and came down again. It was an adventure, and Travice was still like her brother and Dove was glad she had come. There started to be fences, she saw a faraway rash of green that he told her meant wheat. And over there was where their closest neighbours, the Ponts, lived, but you couldn't see their house, it was too far away. Dove was tired, but happy, and he said it wouldn't be long now — home was on that plain dotted with myalls and sandalwoods and native pines. And did Dove see those bushes? — Mr Thorn called them God-damn bushes.

When the Thorns had arrived to take up their land they were everywhere, all prickles, and it was the very devil grubbing them out.

Living in the Mallee had altered Mrs Thorn. Dove was welcomed by a changed lady. Appleton's Mrs Thorn had been proud, even haughty; her eyes had been flinty when they'd seen Dove with Travice. But now Travice's mother had a timid smile and she was so pleased to see Dove. So happy to have a visitor.

It was strange that she lived in an iron house lined with matchboard in the middle of nowhere. Though it was a wonderful place to live, said Travice. You had a better life in the Mallee. Mrs Thorn nodded eagerly, she went trembly as she mimicked agreement. She'd been a woman who'd queened it in Appleton; now she was a mere shadow to her men. When Mr Thorn and George came in she hovered about them, but the Mallee had changed them, too. Somehow they were bigger men, now, and Mrs Thorn was a woman, small — they didn't seem to notice her. Even the fact of Dove's arrival didn't hold their attention for long. The land seemed all they cared about. George smelled different — the furtive rawness Dove remembered had been aired from the frank sweaty smell. Dove decided George Thorn was good-looking. He had grown a beard; he hardly looked at her. But his eyes didn't skid off her in the old frightened way. Now he didn't even appear aware of her. She felt herself begin to act a part — dimple prettily, bite at her lips to make them red. George was no one who counted, but she wanted him to see her.

Issy was the biggest surprise. In Appleton she'd been comical, at her worst on Sundays, striding off to church with a painful expression; someone tortured in her lace collarette, her hat trimmed with imitation grass. Poor

Issy had been a disgrace to her womanhood. Mrs Thorn was always reminding her that anyone with such a large mouth should avoid immoderate laughter and be careful to keep it closed when not speaking. The last time Dove had seen her, she'd looked sillier than usual. Mrs Thorn loved to sew and she'd made Issy a white satin dance dress. There were butterfly bows and accordion pleats and cascades of lace. It was a dress that would have looked charming on any other girl. But, at the final fitting, Issy wouldn't hold her stomach in, she hadn't put on her best corset. The décolletage was demure enough, but Issy's great chest thrust immodestly forward, the bodice hung on her shoulders by a miracle. Issy Thorn had been shameful in duchesse satin. She'd hung her head, while her mother scolded her as if she were a child and went on with the impossible task of bullying the dress right.

But out in the Mallee, Issy had got free. Now she was shameless: she dressed like a man. She wore the same dungarees and faded work-shirt as her father and George; she was as sunburned as a savage — her cheeks were brick red. But she looked tall and healthy and energetic. But it was awful, for she'd cut off her hair. Really, Issy Thorn was a disgrace, but no one except Dove seemed to notice.

Mrs Thorn reminisced constantly of the past. She leaned forward, cradling her head in her hands, and recalled Appleton through a golden haze. Her dreamy voice turned the old days as impossibly soft-centred as the world of a sentimental novel. She couldn't bear to think that Dove's mama was dead, so they sat in the dark and remembered Daisy alive (the curtains were drawn to guard the furniture from the light). In the new drawing-room most things were familiar, but as much altered as their mistress. The piano and twin whatnots were furred with dust, the painted knight and his maiden on the folding screen were almost faded away (it was the harsh Mallee sunlight that had done it), and Mrs Thorn's bamboo gipsy table was covered by a gruesome cloth. It was composed of snakeskins sewn together. Their tails radiated from one snake coiled up in the middle, the pendant heads forming a fringe.

Mrs Thorn sat on the edge of her chair and talked and talked. As she did so, she was continually touching herself — as if she'd just discovered her own body, as if she wanted to remind herself of its existence. She was for ever rubbing at imaginary sore spots; smoothing her temples, stroking her arms, sniffing absently at the backs of her hands. She kept patting her hair and fiddling with the neck and cuff frills of her artistic tea-gown. Its pink satin and ruby plush and old-gold lace elaborations were grubby and quite out-of-date. Ladies didn't wear gowns like that any more — particularly not out in the Mallee — but Mrs Thorn seemed unaware of the fact. She was like someone embalmed, abandoned. Listening to her made Dove feel sad, even though she talked of Appleton so cheerfully. Then, without warning, the sweet voice tapered off to be replaced by an ugly gasping whisper. Mrs Thorn beckoned Dove closer as she confided that she'd been ill. It was the sun that had done it. Summer was coming closer; it would get past the pines that shaded the house to find her again.

Once Mrs Thorn had been wonderful, with eyes that were cords to draw men to her and a voice that could sing them into the islands of the sirens. To Dove, in the old days, she'd been just as good as one of the wicked diamond-strewn ladies who'd featured in her favourite

76

novels. But now she was merely pathetic, with a faraway look in her eyes and a wistful smile. Dove felt sorry for Mrs Thorn, but she couldn't help scorning her, too. The skin that had been warmly white, like the petals of a white rose, was lemon-coloured and Dove stared moodily at the drawing-room carpet and hated Mrs Thorn for ending up defeated with wrinkles, and knew that it could never happen to her. Even Rosa and Will had the guts to row and make a fuss, but Mrs Thorn was so bright, so purposefully cheery, while all the time she was moaning inside.

But once past the drawing-room, Dove was surrounded by an adventure. The country was open, so free. It spread out before her, it had no secrets to hide like the Hills. Dove was far from pebble-dash and pittosporum — she never wanted to go back. She was tired of walking trapped on a false crust of footpath; she wanted to stay here with the great fields of wheat — and this was White Tuscan, soft and sweet, a hay wheat that horses relished ... and Federation and Silver King were other sorts ... and this was Le Huguenot that grew nearly six feet high ...

And was the earth pink or orange? It was a pale poppy colour, a soft chalky red. The colours were so mild, yet the restlessness of spring was everywhere. It speared the pinky-red earth with juicy green wheat stalks; it was in the swift moving clouds, the teasing wind. Dove's eyes saw freshly, her head felt clear. She knew who she was and she never wanted to leave. With axe and slasher, scrub roller and stump-jump plough, the Thorns were heroes who'd created a landscape. They had changed the colour of a country.

●●●

It was splendid to be together again. Who'd have thought they were both eighteen? It seemed they were still two children — everything they did was fun.

Travice got the football out and they kicked it to each other on the plain, and Dove rode the bike round and round, but she went too fast and got the wobbles and ended up in the dam. And he showed her the big gum tree where the white cockatoos always settled; and it was a great place for lizards, from little ones up to goannas. They were all spikes and thorns and projections. One sort carried a peculiar little hump at the back of its head and had the power of changing colour; another, when Travice held it up, struggled free and scurried away, leaving its tail behind in his fingers.

Dove liked everything about Travice; he was so tall and straight and brown. She knew the smell of his skin, and the way his mouth trembled when he smiled. She never wanted him any different. He was a boy, bright and alive, while most people were sleepy and stupid. He was so funny, walking gravely beside her like a regular city gentleman in his straw hat. He was proud of that hat, he thought it smart; he didn't know that hard-hitters were out, that men in the city had a mad fit for wearing soft Panamas.

He showed her the vegetable garden he'd made in a stretch of red loam that lay between the sand-hills. He grew tomatoes and carrots, cabbages and lettuces. Nearby were several clingstone peach trees.

In the evening after tea they sat in the drawing-room and had a concert. Mrs Thorn appeared almost her old self as she played the piano for their sing-song. Travice held Dove's hand all night.

If you stood on a Mallee sand-hill you were likely to tread on anything. As well as spear-grass and spinifex and bluebush and the beady-eyed lizards, there were stick-insects that looked just like the twig of a bush, and crackerjack beetles that tucked their legs in and shammed dead if you touched them. But you never meddled with a redback spider; you had nothing to do with a snake.

Shell parrots flew overhead in a green cloud and the robins were beauties — somehow in the Mallee their breasts seemed a brighter red, but about the gum trees the wheat was bent and broken down by the white cockatoos which did no little damage to the crops. At night the big brown owl came round the haystack watching for mice. The weird whistle of the curlew sent shivers down Dove's spine.

And Travice told her about clearing the scrub with the great roller that was pulled by seven horses. When they'd finished with it, they sold it to Uncle Harold Thorn who lived further north. He brought a bullock team down with him to fetch it, but he'd never driven bullocks before and they were tying themselves in knots, because with bullocks you must wave the whip the right way. If you waved *this* way they came round *that* way, but Uncle Harold did it wrong — the leader was always at the back instead of the front.

A wheat farm mean new words. *Rust* and *smut*, *bunt* and *take-all* were diseases that struck at your crop; cocky-chaff was the husk of the wheat-head that was separated from the grain with the winnower and fed, mixed with molasses and oats, to the horses.

The cocky-chaff shed stood between the straw-roofed stable and the haystack. When they went in, Dove could hardly see. Chaff spilled out from the galvanized iron walls; there was a hot stuffy smell and she didn't know what those machines were down the end, but their jumbled shapes looked sinister. Suddenly Travice had stopped being her friend, he was a stranger as he grasped her shoulders and leaned against her. He was holding her tight, his hands were hurting her, and once by the mulberry tree he'd kissed her properly — his mouth had been neat and pursed, but now he did it wrong, she couldn't bear it.

·

Travice was the captain of the local football team. On the Saturday before Dove left, she watched him play.

The oval was a sober wasteland of creamy-grey stubble, tufted here and there with a try at green. The little town it belonged to was as disappointing. They'd passed merely a general store and a blacksmith's shop, a row of cottages for the gang that was working to extend the railway line.

But it was an outing, an event. Preparations had been going on since sun-up. Dusty buggies had been washed down, harnesses cleaned, hoofs trimmed. Best dresses, smelling strongly of moth-ball, had been taken from their drawers and carefully pressed. You were judged to be a gentlewoman by what you wore on your head and Dove saw hats shaped like scallop-shells and flower pots, candle extinguishers and mushrooms. Mrs Thorn outdid all the other ladies with her trimmings of pigeon's wings and artificial snowballs, the spider's web pattern of her veil. You showed off your frizzed fringe, your magpie shoes of black and white leather, your impossible scarlet silk stockings. The sun shone, there was a mingled scent of lavender water, macassar oil and Yankee Doodle tobacco, and gentlemen blazed in a brassy twinkle of watch-chains and tie-pins, signet rings and polished boots. There were assorted thickets of beards and side whiskers; a luxuriance of bicycle-handle moustaches. Hankies peeped from breast pockets, straw hats were worn at jaunty angles; there were all manner of floral snippets in buttonholes.

At first Dove, in her simple white dress and Wattle Day hat, thought them ridiculous — then she saw them as people who were brave. Their fingers were seamed with hard toil, their faces were dry and leathery, but they still had the spunk to dress up — even Mrs Thorn in her ruin. They were ordinary and earthbound, yet they stood so proudly, so pitifully English (all unknowingly years and years out of fashion) hedged by an antipodean jungle of stiff splintered branches, a mysterious pearly-grey gloom. The wheat fields had only spread so far; the untamed Mallee country seemed endless.

Into the hot sunshine of the quiet clearing drove up buggy after buggy, a few sulkies, and riders in twos and threes. Soon, under every shady tree, was tied a sweat-stained horse, and saddle and harness, hampers, rugs and billies cumbered the ground in all directions. Groups of people gathered to chat, and Dove felt important as she was introduced as a friend of the Thorns from the city. But the girl called Enid Pont didn't like her — Dove sensed her distaste straight away.

Enid was a tall girl, droopy. Her thick black hair was freshly washed, its antiseptic smell reminded Dove of pimple cream. She was a nice girl, as pale and good as a Sunday School teacher. But she didn't like Dove. Her eyes were too polite; her rabbity mouth smiled too carefully, kindly. Something was wrong. The sweat beads along her upper lip made a little moustache; her hands were clenched tight.

She was Issy's friend and Dove's mouth curled.

Doubtless Enid was another girl who'd never get married; she was the sort who wouldn't know how to flirt or dimple or fake at being the sweet fool that was a man's undoing. Though she'd got herself up nicely enough for the football, almost as if she had someone in mind. Her hair made a frizzy black tower under the brim of her tilted gable bonnet; she kept pulling at her stays as if she weren't used to wearing them; she'd pinned a cluster of forget-me-nots to her bodice.

Dove supposed, grudgingly, that Enid was attractive ... and it must be comforting to have a best friend ... Issy Thorn looked almost handsome with her tanned face and blow-about hair. She was so brown and strong and sturdy, yet where her collar fell back from her neck, the skin was delicately pale, vulnerable ... The insides of her arms, where her sleeves rolled back, were smooth and white, too ...

The ground was really only a grazing paddock, having an appreciable fall north-south and dipping alarmingly on the western wing. Some yards on to the oval itself, between one of the half forward flanks and the goal area, stood a large tree.

Then it was Hoo-jolly-ray! and the game had begun, though to begin with it meant only country boys of various shapes and sizes running about, whooping and calling for a kick to come their way, and a ball that was snatched at, that hovered elusive in the air. For a while he was only Travice — her companion from childhood, almost her brother, though he'd held her hand through the sing-song and kissed her in that unpleasant way in the shed; though she'd never seen his legs above knee before, and in his football clothes he looked older, more man than boy ... though his team's guernseys were so bright, their red and green stripes contested so viciously with each other that it quite hurt Dove's eyes to look.

But it was good standing there smelling the turfy earthy smell, with the sun on her face and the sky arching overhead like a rumpled satin eiderdown that kept miraculously changing its colour — now it was blue, then blue-grey, then grey with the silvery sheen of a new shilling. The sun came closer, Dove was cocooned in a golden haze of content, and her identity — and the others', too — slipped away: now she only knew the people about her as voices, blurred shapes. The voices joined together; they blended in Dove's head. Nothing seemed to matter but the scurrying figures on the oval, playing out their queer ritual. People's faces were different, too. They'd come prepared, dressed in their best, for it was a masquerade where fantasy overtook them and passion was in their voices, their faces. The women had discarded their accepting faces of everyday; for the length of each quarter they were allowed to love those raw bodies, to hate and berate and harangue.

Mrs Thorn threw back her veil to see better and the pigeon's wings and snowballs were masked with sombre cobwebs, and it seemed she wore a miniature mausoleum on her head. Her yellowy face had lost its passive look of hopeless dreaming; her profile was sharp and cruel as: "Miss ... miss ... miss ... " she hissed, witchlike, as the enemy aimed for its goal. And Issy was ruddy and brave, for she felt that she ran on the oval with them. She was just a body, too, bathed in sweat, that embraced, was embraced, as the goal umpire's flag fluttered and the score crept on. The women watched, and all their secret passion got free — they were savage, they had the smell of them, as they called for their blood. When it came it was beautiful. It was a giant poppy blooming on the chalky clown face. He bled so red. The poppy's petals shivered, quivered, until the flower was shredded away.

But it was only a blood nose. It wasn't war or romance — only a game of footer and this one was like an old woman at a christening, that one was a goose who'd run out of puff.

At half-time the rival team's supporters sent the scores back to their home town by homing pigeon.

When the game began again, Enid Pont pressed forward and began to call Travice's name, to barrack as if he were hers. Suddenly they were calling together — Dove and Enid. Their voices fought for him; it was as if their calls hung on to Travice with little hooks and tried to catch him as he ran on the oval's stamped earth. It was only a game with a ball, but it was as thrilling as those times when Mr Thorn had killed a pig. Now Dove saw them as men — some in red and green, others in black and white — with their shadows running beside them; then their shadows tangled, massed, and they were giants that grappled and clashed in the sky. Travice had escaped to be just a body — he leaped highest of all. He was hero-anonymous; a man labelled only by the number on his back, leaping free of his past and his life off the oval. He'd stopped being awkward; his body had grace. He leaped, he fell at the air. It was as if he died in the sky for a moment; it was like poetry: the still jump, the frozen moment. Then the roar of the crowd was a wind that blew its great *Ahhh* ... It blew him alive again, and the ball fell into his hands.

Years later, Dove remembered it as the most romantic part of their courtship. Though he was nowhere near her, though someone else called his name, too. It was the other girl wanting him that made the moment perfect. Dove knew he was worth having then. She wanted him so much. If his body coming close must be part of it, she would have that as well; she would even bear Mrs Thorn. As Travice kicked the ball between the posts, and the red and green goal was cheered, Dove made up her mind that they'd be married.

After the game was over, billies and saddle-quarts were filled at a creek and soon the blue, sweet-scented smoke was curling up from a dozen little fires of dry twigs and gum leaves. Coats were shed, hampers opened, and groups of old friends settled down to eat and exchange news of the births, marriages and deaths of the district.

The weird black bush shadows lengthened. One after another horses were yoked and saddled, goodbyes said, and then brakes rasped as the buggies drove away. With mysterious rapidity moonlight replaced the last glimmer of day. Only the faint, clinging smell of smoke from the picnic fires was a reminder of the day's meetings and greetings about the oval.

But some people went on to a dance in the hall that stood on a nearby hill, familiarly called Paradise, on account of being so high up and difficult to reach.

The Germans from the railway gang played their accordions, and Dove danced with Travice, they spun round and round on the floor that had been polished with candle wax. The big hurricane lanterns blazed above their heads, there were streamers and flowers, and they did the Alberts, the Lancers, the polka mazurka, the waltz. Enid Pont was dancing with George. The forget-me-nots on her bodice were sadly wilted.

Five

"My fiancé," Dove said proudly and showed off the ring as much as his photo. It meant glitter and romance and Travice's likeness was nice, too. Dear thing. She loved his innocent artless expression, his head cocked to one side. He smiled in the old familiar way and he was beautifully turned out; he was a dandy in his waistcoat and flower buttonhole.

She loved him, but she looked past the photo face and saw the ideal. Safely distanced, he stayed that hero who'd leaped at the sky. When they'd danced his hand had felt sweaty, he trod on her feet. But it didn't matter — she was engaged to be married, she'd selected her trousseau. Rosa reckoned they were too young, but Dove tossed her head. It was a way to escape. Mrs Thorn had her measurements, and had started on the wedding-dress already. Dove walked about feeling protected. For the Mallee's stiff trees walked with her, they hedged her mind all the time, and because of it she was someone, she had something to talk about when ladies called. Once Dove's head had been empty, for the Hills had disappeared and the landscape that took their place belonged to Rosa. Once she'd been so pale she was almost invisible — she'd known she was boring and her mouth felt unused. But now Dove was as much an ideal as Travice and the Mallee. She was someone important, for she was getting married. The ladies from the church sank back against Rosa's art serge cushions and Dove did her performance, she was as fetching as the spangled circus girl on the galloping horse as she read from his letters.

Dove sent Travice a photo in return — she was in white, with a big hat and her hair loose, and flowers at the throat, ruffles and pin-tucks, and then the great bell sleeves, the bell of skirt. And Dove knew which wheats were good yielders and how you didn't use manures on virgin soil and oh, it would be an adventure and she saw her life bathed in the soft glow of paraffin lamps; saw herself moving about all misty amongst the prime plump grain of a record harvest and she said the names of the wheats — Federation, Silver King — as if they were old friends. It was a fair land where Dove was bound for, and she boasted about the bore, the oil engine, the pump and storage tanks and the hay waggons with their over-hanging sweet-scented loads and somehow the story she told was muddled with Mama's tales of Arden Valley. Dove couldn't help it — it wasn't lying, not even pretending, for she believed it, she saw it, she really did. Even as she described a land of the golden fleece, pre-cious metals, waving corn — of wine and oil, milk and honey, she saw the old lady like Queen Victoria, the little boy in his Lord Fauntleroy suit.

It could have been a city wedding in Rosa's church but Dove had adopted the Mallee, it took the place of the Hills, it meant she belonged. So the Priddles waved goodbye, and then she was in the train again and Travice was there to meet her with the buggy. It was then that things started going wrong. They drove the forty miles and summer was over, harvest was done, it was autumn and nothing was the same. The land was all black; the wheat stubble had been burned and it was like taking a journey in Hell. Dove came out of her dream: it seemed a funny thing to be doing — driving through a charred landscape to marry a stranger. For she felt she didn't know him — he was ordinary, not a hero: he was only her friend. And was it true what the church ladies had whispered? — about demands that could not be restrained, and how your body wasn't your own.

But it was as good as done; she had that many wedding presents. She had a brush and comb, an eiderdown, vases ...

So Dove's wedding-dress was white satin, her going-away frock was purple silk. And she had a long purple coat and buttoned boots and she married Travice in the marquee by the shed. After the wedding breakfast there was dancing and carryings on. Issy chased the minister and put rice down his back; George played handies with Enid.

They spent their honeymoon at the town by the river and Dove was a country girl, she knew what was what — but it was nothing to do with her. For a nice girl knew that the stork brought the baby, though you might also find one under a cabbage. But they slept in the same bed and she didn't know if he was frightened, or if she was frightened, or what. He kissed her in the awful way and she pushed him off and then he didn't touch her, but wasn't he supposed to, wasn't there something that had to break, didn't she have to bleed or something?

She had no one to ask and they'd stopped being friends. It was better in the daytime when they walked by the river, under the willows. The other guests thought it sweet and even in the evenings it wasn't too bad. Nothing was so beautiful as the river boat coming in ablaze with lights, just as dinner finished. The whistle would sound and everyone would go down to the wharf to see her edge in. Dove knew the right way to feel —

she knew she was privileged to have lived to see all that beauty. The river called her like a magnet. She didn't want to go back to the hotel room for another night of lying side by side.

Dove had never had anything much to do with babies and she didn't know very much about having them. She thought they had to cut you down the front to have one, she really did. She said to Issy: "How will I know when the baby's coming?" Issy said: "You'll know all right," and looked grim. But Issy was only a character; she was a dear old thing, her bark was worse than her bite (it was the way Dove was determined to see her, she *would* have Issy like that). Dove made her voice sweeter than ever as she tried again: "Well, how does it come out — do they cut you right down the tummy?" she asked and then it was lovely, it was dreadful. Dove had her reward — Issy couldn't take any more, her voice was harsh. "No," she said, "it bloody well comes out the same way as it got in."

Dove was determined to stay ladylike. She was in a certain state, yes, but she would say the right words, she would keep on pretending. She wouldn't recall how Mama had hinted that it hadn't exactly been a picnic when she lay by the stone angel in the grounds of Arden House; how Rosa had gone through all that grunting and groaning with Ralph.

Dove kept on being clever, she pretended innocence so well. It went on being nothing to do with her — that queer swollen thing that her stomach had become. But she took her revenge. She had a good way of looking at Travice — sort of saintly-sorrowful; and she sighed, and was constantly running away from the table, even when there wasn't anything to sick up. She would show him it was his fault; that she would never forgive him for cheating her, by having his way. For in the end, at the hotel by the river, she'd pitied him ... and she'd been curious, too. But how could it be Dove he did it to, who let him do it? How did doing *that* fit into a world of *good mornings* and *beg pardons*, of rules where it was a bad girl who wore a low cut flesh-pink blouse, a good girl who was buttoned up to her whalebone collar? Dove's daytime collars were proper but night turned her into a body that liked what he did. In the morning it was something they didn't refer to, though the pictures in her head were shameful. He squeezed her hand, and looked at her sentimentally. She knew she wouldn't let him do it again, but when night came she was the bad girl in his arms. It was like dividing into two, and all the other pairs of people must do it, and every other wife seemed to manage the two parts. Somehow Dove couldn't. She felt more and more muddled and ashamed. She wanted to be fresh and unsoiled, Travice had made her soul feel dirty. She would go to Papa's Hell, she knew; the Tin Tabernacle's warnings of perdition were terrible.

She was wicked, but when Bobby was born they said she was brave. But they couldn't read her mind, they didn't know she was screaming inside. Though she didn't make a sound. She lay there quiet through the hurting, pretending she didn't feel a thing. Issy said why didn't she call out — her face kept swimming close; Issy's eyes were beautiful, they were as soft as jelly, but her hard hands tormented Dove's body and it was like a butcher's shop and Mrs Thorn's face was there, too. The men's voices were low behind the door. "Scream if it helps," said Issy, but Dove's mouth stayed shut though it was like being tortured by demons and Mrs Thorn's face was a frightened glossy yellow. Nothing normal could be born in this way to the dresses with their baby ribbon, the shell-stitch shawl. But Dove would believe, she *would* — about under the cabbage, the rose bush ... how perhaps you'd have a baby because he kissed you. But everything was stained and slippery. It was the mulberry fight, when her pinafore told the story and Mama said it would never come clean. She had to soak it for ages, but they were lovely as a table dessert with sugar and cream. Why, picking mulberries could even be romantic. It wasn't only fights, it could be a lovers' paradise up the tree. Travice and Dove often picked mulberries on the same branch ...

Having a baby seemed the most horrid thing in the world. All through it Dove thought she would die, though she knew that sort of thinking to be wrong. It was immodest, indelicate, it didn't mean a thing. Nothing she did could be important: it was just having a baby, and it happened to every mother and Dove was one now — but, really, she was no one. Being Mrs Thorn who lived in the Mallee was too difficult. She couldn't play the part right. She might have stayed Miss Sparks, for she was still pale, and worried because she didn't fit in. The worries were little stitches nipping at her mind, sewing her tighter into her feeling of not existing. She only came alive when her night-time body got free — it had got her into this, she was ashamed.

Then somehow the pain was over; somewhere a baby cried. They said she had a fine big son: it was Bobby, but Dove didn't know him then ... then, she didn't feel anything: she didn't want to see the child. But she had to. It was part of Little Mother's role.

Baby went into her arms, but all the uglier evidence of

her hurting was tidied away. They wiped off the sweat that might have been death damps, and combed out her hair. Appearances must be kept up, for what had happened was a woman's secret. When they let the men in, Travice seemed further away than ever. He looked at her across a great distance as if she were holy.

After the child was born their life together was better. Being Bobby's mother was an excuse to keep the bad girl away. Travice and Dove were friends again. At night, in the big stone room that was theirs at the back of the house, they were gentle with each other.

Bobby was a beautiful child, always so good. He was as fat as butter and filled his nightdresses up; he had his mother's fair hair and blue eyes. When Dove held him in her arms at the football match, people turned round to look at him.

Travice didn't play now. There was too much to do on the farm. His red and green guernsey had ended its days of usefulness disfiguring the landscape on a scarecrow's back.

Sometimes Dove felt like a sleepwalker — there was no time to think. She supposed she was happy. The Thorns didn't annoy her so much: it didn't seem to matter about Mr Thorn's habit of spitting and the noise he made when he ate; or Mrs Thorn's vagueness and her dusty drawing-room, her rag-tag assortment of finery; or how George hardly spoke and, when he did, his nose puffed in and out, his voice sounded squawky. Even Issy's mannishness was something Dove had learned to accept. Since Bobby's birth, they'd stopped needling each other. If it hadn't been for Issy, Dove might have died.

But it was a queer life. They were afraid every spring, even though the wheat stood up brave and green. Weather meant all — anything could happen. Now it was friend, then enemy. They watched the sky anxiously for rain; a hot wind was a disaster; the sky could suddenly turn dark, dust blew, and the sunflowers lashed back and forth like giant pendulums.

Dove had a garden. She kept the flowers alive with dishwater over summer. Even the slip of honeysuckle had taken. It was Bobby's favourite — he always pointed to the honeysuckle.

Summer was awful — the Mallee was the devil's country, then — but a lady wore her corset all through it. They used to put a tub of water down the cellar and go there and bathe. Mrs Thorn looked comical with her pearls round her neck and her clothes off, her legs sticking over the side. But summer was when she was a trial. She so much dreaded letting any ray of sunshine touch her skin, that she hastened to the lavatory under a large sunshade of holland lined with green. And though the curtains were drawn, she was always peering through the gloom into mirrors to ascertain that her old antagonist was outwitted. But summer meant harvest, and it was when Dove must help with the winnowing.

The wheat from the stripper had been emptied into a heap and the winnower was alongside it, and then they fed it in and the clean wheat fell through the sieves, while the wind from the big fan blew the cocky-chaff and rubbish away. Dove helped fill up the bags. She had a pick handle to ram the grain in, so the bags would fill up nice and tight. She had a wheat bag round her neck and stockings on her arms so she wouldn't get sunburned. But her hands still went red, and there were fine lines of black on her palms that she had to scrub and scrub at to remove.

The Mallee was a great place for flies. The sandflies stung and bit until they drew blood. They clustered in the corners of the horses' eyes, drinking the tears.

One year there was a mouse plague. They came in thousands, the haystack was moving. They ate holes in the wheat bags; the cocky-chaff shed was full of them. Somehow they got into the house, and one started eating Issy's fingernail through the night — it took the end clean off. But the haystack was the worst place. George dug a trench round it, and put in some kerosene tins of water. In the morning the tins were full of drowned mice, while there were other mice, alive, running over the top of each other, fighting to escape. Like the plagues of Egypt, they just came (but where did they come from?). Then they passed on — somehow they disappeared.

But there were always rabbits eating the wheat: the men were constantly shooting them and going out with the poison cart. The horses used to pull it over the sandhills; it held pollard and poison, mixed to a stiff paste, and was fixed up with this little affair on the bottom that made a furrow and dropped pieces out. Wherever the cart went the place was thick with dead rabbits. The smell was awful.

The loneliness was there all the time, too. The house stood on the plain surrounded by mallee trees and pines. From the house they couldn't even see the wheat fields; through the trees they could only see one sand-hill (Dove knew its shape by heart). The men and Issy set off for the fields on the trolley, and then Dove was alone with Bobby and Mrs Thorn. Every morning, the first thing they did was to trim the lamps.

Few people came; the Afghan hawker's visit was an occasion. Dove felt excited when she saw the small cloud of dust growing bigger on the road and knew that he was coming in his buggy. He had a turban and magpie eyes. His goods were tawdry but they always bought something and invited him in to drink tea. He was a man from the outside world who'd seen *The Dollar Princess* at the Theatre Royal, and knew that the two-step had ousted the waltz. Mrs Thorn dusted the piano keys with her hanky and got out her music. He listened politely as she played "Fly Away Birdie to Heaven" and "Mansion of Aching Hearts".

Then it was 1914, when it just didn't rain and didn't rain and didn't rain. They'd put in five hundred acres that year, a fair lump of ground, but they'd just wasted the seed. It didn't rain and the wheat frizzled up and the fowls were getting round with their mouths wide open; the tanks were dry, the horses starving. They took down the straw from the roof of the stable and chaffed it up and fed it with molasses to the stock to try and save them. But the animals kept dying. Mr Thorn had given Bobby a foal, and the poor little beggar finished up eating mallee bark. If you didn't have it, you couldn't give it to them. He died, that foal, poor sod.

There'd be grey mornings, with a sort of drifting shifting mist over everything — all the outlines blurred, as in a water-colour, and the distance guessed at; a sort of brooding quiet, through which the voices of a few birds came almost startlingly. The rest were hushed like the morning — waiting. The great clouds came day by day, only to go away again; the Ponts spent day after day going round breaking the necks of their sheep. They did not bleat, it was a kind of moan you had to listen for.

They were half-eaten by the crows sometimes, but still alive.

It didn't rain until September, and by that time there was a war. There was disaster all through the Mallee, but the supreme crime was committed when Rheims Cathedral was destroyed. When the newpaper came there was a race to see if the Germans had got to Calais, whether the Russians were still advancing.

Now, all over the outback, when mail was delivered at the wayside letterboxes nailed sometimes to a post, as often to a tree, a horseman would usually be waiting to hear the latest war news. The pith of it could just be given as the mailman hunted through his bag for letters and papers or handed over a parcel or cog, or some other new part for a harvester or windmill pump. Then the mailman was off and the horseman, cantering back through the scrub, would be wondering if the next week's news would be good or bad, and if he should go down and enlist with the Light Horse.

When the German *Emden* was sunk by the Australian cruiser, *Sydney*, off Cocos Island, there was general rejoicing. The drought, starving horses, poor crops and dry tanks were for a time forgotten. Youths who had never seen a city, who had never been more than perhaps fifty miles from their native town, were bubbling over with the news and elated at the achievement. George Thorn was no youngster, and he was as good as engaged to Enid Pont, but: "I am going to enlist," he said, "there is nothing doing here."

Across the world was the great adventure, and at the recruiting meeting when the Colonel cried "Eligibles! Follow me!" George stood up. His patriotism was in contrast to that of his brother. When Dove had told Travice about the *Emden*, he'd merely shrugged and gone on talking about how Ponts' dog had arrived with a note round its neck to say that their sow had died. Dove had married a stay-at-home. Battleships and wars were of no interest to Travice.

George went into camp with a real good mob, only he did not think much of the Cheer-up Society ladies — they had faces on them to crack a whisky bottle. He gave Enid his gold sleeve links made into a brooch, and she gave him a kangaroo trinket, a mascot he promised to treasure and bring safely home from the war.

Cairo was not much of a place. George wrote that in the native parts it was very dirty, and the tarts were in hundreds — "but not for me thank you." The Egyptians were dirty devils, most of them didn't wear hat or boot, though some were flashies. There were a terrible lot of Greeks in all the towns. You didn't see a white face very often except the soldiers and nurses.

Then he was well in the firing line and had joined the machine guns but couldn't describe the place as it wasn't allowed (his letters were written in pencil, the envelopes were stamped PASSED BY CENSOR); but he was "somewhere in France" where beer was a penny a glass and he heard some pretty good yarns; but the mud was terrible, the return journey seemed a hell of a long way off. And George Thorn shot a German — he was sure of it, he saw him fall — and sent home some foreign coins, and a hanky embroidered with the flags of the Allies, and a pair of bullet-shells joined together to hold needles. But by the time they arrived George had been killed in action. On the memoriam card it said:

He fell! a hero in the deadly strife,
For King and Country he laid down his life,
Fame was achieved, and he had done his share
To win those laurels, rich and rare,
Which now adorn Australia's loyal race,
Not even Time! its glory can efface.

Six

There was a page in the newspaper called "Life's Tragic Side", and every paragraph had a heading: "A Dog-cart Capsized", "Poisoned by Wedding-cake" ... It comforted Dove to read it. She might be stuck in the Mallee, but she was safe. Other lives in other worlds were more risky: it made her day just to read of them. It was better than the war news, for the uniforms made them strangers and one expected a soldier to die, after all. But these deaths stayed real. It might have been Dove who fell on her head or got sunstruck. Because it wasn't, she felt guarded by God.

But then He stopped playing fair. Travice came out of the house and opened his arms and Bobby began to run towards him, but tripped and fell and broke the blood vessel in his heart and died in seconds.

Once Travice Thorn had been different. He was a joker, full of mischief, but kind. He wouldn't hunt the nocturnal possum; when the cow was sick he sat up with her all night. But the Mallee had changed him. Now he was serious, unsmiling; he worked so hard, he was always tired. And he went out with the poison cart, he shot the jays that pecked at the new wheat stalks; when he burned the stubble a fox emerged from the flames singed from the tip of its tail to the end of its nose. He killed the bullock; he killed the sheep. What did it feel like doing it? — Dove wanted to know. He shrugged and said you sort of got used to it.

Dove wouldn't believe Bobby was gone at first. She gathered him in her arms and his cheeks were rosy, he smelled of spear-grass. He was her darling and she wouldn't let the Thorns come near. She put a hot brick to his feet and cold compresses to his forehead. But he was dead, and he was only three years old. The honey-suckle had somehow survived the drought and Bobby loved its flowers, so Dove put a piece in his hand before he was buried.

She went round smelling his clothes. And there was his cup on the shelf. And there were the corals that he used to play with. He sucked them, bit them.

Dove had played with the coral necklace before him. It had been a fairy godmother's present, part of her personal legend. Dove had been born, once upon a time, in a grand house, in a secret valley — she was a chosen child from her beginning. Once, magic had been all about her. It had seemed like it to Dove, anyway, when Mama spoke of Arden Valley.

In the Mallee, Dove was still a listener. Mrs Thorn rambled on, and the legend was reduced to how Uncle Harold waved the bullock whip wrong ... the mice plague, the drought ...

One day Bobby would be part of a legend, too. People wouldn't feel a thing as they told how he'd been a little boy like an angel. But Dove didn't want him that way — she wanted him flawed. He'd been a nuisance, sometimes, building cubby-houses from cushions, always following her round, tormenting her with his silly babble.

But Bobby fell. There was blood from his nose.

Travice had made it happen, but he didn't seem to care. Issy took Dove aside and said he mightn't show it, but he would never get over it. He was Dove's husband, but Issy was trying to explain him. She looked at Dove curiously, her mouth said one thing but her eyes said another. Dove knew that Issy thought Travice should have married Enid Pont. Issy treated Enid like a heroine because George had been killed in the war. Why couldn't it have been Travice who'd gone off in khaki? Then Dove would have been the one accepting Issy's homage.

After Bobby died Dove couldn't bear to stay in the house with Mrs Thorn. A panicky feeling came and she had to get away. But she knew she was caught, that they had her — and she would end up faded and silly, and the loneliness beat against her like giant wings until she felt sick with fear. Mrs Thorn kept watching her as she clattered the knives and forks into their drawer; she kept clearing her throat nervously as if she had something to say. Dove would go mad if she didn't escape. But the new baby was coming, though it could never make up for Bobby: Dove would stay in the Mallee for ever. Soon they would start on the lamps. Mrs Thorn would get out the box that held the soft mop for chimney cleaning, the tissue paper, scissors, funnel, duster. Dove couldn't bear it she ran outside.

The tufted bushes were pincushions, tiny tufted islands in the pink sandy soil. Here and there dead boughs were neatly piled (the land seemed to mock her, it was nothing like the Hills) — and who had made these neat piles of sticks, why were they here?

The light was so bright. It meant she must walk with her eyes screwed up, until her face ached. And she couldn't escape by looking at the sky. The light pinned her down. She was trapped on the orange earth, kept low. Now she wanted everything that she'd scorned: the butcher in his striped apron, the draper in his celluloid collar ... but more than anything she wanted the Hills. She wanted to creep away, hide where no eye could find her; be the child Dove safe in the cave of Mama's skirts. Travice had cheated her; he was a pretender, an imposter without loyalty to their shared past. He'd taken her further from the old days than ever; even the drought couldn't prise him from the wheat-land. But worst of all: Travice had killed Bobby.

She walked over leaves and bark and shadows. But it was dull, dull — it was *their* sky and earth, and everything was second-rate, second-hand, and dull resentment weighed her down. But sometimes peace would nibble at her soul, and the Mallee seem almost beautiful. There was a patch of scrub where everlastings grew; and, where the plough had been, the pale surface of the earth turned up to reveal its ripe red underside. But Dove didn't want peace; she wouldn't turn monstrous like the Thorns. She wasn't an animal to accept, to not feel (Bobby had died, she would never forget). She saw the everlastings but, then, tramping over the sand-hills, there was the smell: the poison cart had been there before her, the earth was crusted with dead rabbits. Only the Hills were perfect. The Mallee was a nightmare place, so placid as it endured. She was antlike with the sky breathing on her, the whispery wheat-heads spreading about her. The furrows curved in great arcs and Dove was enclosed.

Often she walked until the day softened into evening. Smoky shadows thickened, spread. There was stillness, silence and pink tones, pearly, in the earth; gold tints on tree trunks. Once, at sunset, the clouds made a fiery eagle in the sky — rosy-winged, poised. The land, then, was tinged with plum. It was an ancient masquerader as mauve colours crept into fence posts and the sky, for a time, was a delicate lilac. It was a frail dreaming land, and all the bushes stood out goldeny. Then the brown-mauves took over and the furrowed earth was velvety, plushy. But Dove wasn't big enough to match the land. She was small; she wanted the clenched hills that had hedged and hidden her.

Dove hardly saw Travice, now, because there was so much work to be done on the farm. It was seeding-time and he got up early, in the wintry morning dark, and came home when it was dark again. A cycle had begun, the year kept moving on. Dove stood still while the seasons passed over her. Soon it would be another harvest and she would have another child.

But it wouldn't be born in the Mallee. Remembering Bobby, Dove made up her mind: they'd go back to the Hills.

When she told Travice, he said he couldn't leave his mother. Now George was gone, she needed him more than ever. And what about the farm? His father and Issy couldn't work it without him.

Behind his words was the Mallee. It was a terrible place for making money, but somehow he enjoyed the life. It meant being out in the blue morning, and the way the beaters in the stripper went round like billyoh, and the bloke who just came and pitched his tent and could play tunes on a gum leaf ... Travice didn't say any of it, he stayed silent, but Dove could hear his voice going on, she could see their life stretching ahead. He couldn't understand why she didn't fit in. Why couldn't she be like Enid Pont? George had died, but it didn't stop Enid smiling and winning the sugar bowl for the best lady rider at the sports day.

Travice belonged in the Mallee, it had taken the place of the Hills as his home. He even liked the worst days of summer because the hotter it was for reaping, the better; though it was hard on the horses, poor beggars, with the sandflies nearly eating them; but he used to change the teams about dinner-time, take four out of the stripper, put another four in. There was always something to be done — he was going to build a special house for the incubator, for hatching out chickens (he sent the eggs to town, but they were robbers down there; they only paid fivepence a dozen and always reckoned that some eggs had blood in them, others were broken). And there were the wheats — Federation with its dark brown heads that held their grain in storms; Le Huguenot that was tall. Remember: God-damn bushes, sandalwoods, shell parrots, owls, and that bird like a quail, but bigger; and the lizards, the saltbush, bluebush ...

Dove knew these things were in his head, though all he said, dreamily, as if he were thinking aloud, was that it was a risky business and what about that chap who shot himself, God knows why, but probably it was the drought that got him down. But it was a good life; though you could lose all you had — you'd have two good crops, then a bad one. But it was a wonderful place to live.

She told him again that they must leave, but he looked at her as if he didn't understand. So it was her turn to remember, the words spilled out. About lilies by the creek, the wattles, the apple trees. Dove was of age, she had her share of the money from Papa's dying and it would go towards a new home at Appleton.

Mrs Thorn would drive Dove mad. She was ugly, with the spit coming out of her mouth and she had a smell about her — Travice defended his mother, he said the smell was to do with her sickness, but it was just an excuse. She was an old lady pretending, too lazy to wash, and when she moved the stink moved with her. It was rich and fruity, so alive, but it came out of her dried up body. She was as skinny as a skeleton leaf but the smell was always there, itchy and excited, under her rag-bag gown and Dove saw a cockroach run out of her skirt and she wouldn't end up like Mrs Thorn — no never. But she might. For it was the Mallee that had turned Mrs Thorn odd. The aloneness had done it and she'd been worse lately, even though it was winter and she couldn't blame the sun. Mrs Thorn had a new habit. She'd sit hunched, cradling her elbows, and then slowly her fingers would start to edge up. She felt up her arms: she reckoned she felt knobs — they went all the way to her heart. The number of knobs kept increasing and she'd predicted the day she would die, but why didn't she get on with it, why must the date stay always somewhere ahead? Dove was tired of the old lady's whining and why was she alive, why had it been Bobby in the little white coffin lined with satin? It had silver on the handles, it was the best they could get, and he lay there dressed in white like a little marble carving with the honeysuckle in his hand and, since he'd died, part of Dove was the frantic fluttering thing, but another part of her was flinty and cold. She stayed hard and hating, un-pitying, as Mrs Thorn looked at Travice with tears in her eyes because he was all she had now that George had given his life and Issy had gone like a man and Mr Thorn, with his belching and farting, like one of the pigs. Once they'd been proper people. It was the Mallee that had altered them all.

But it wouldn't get Dove, even if to escape meant using Bobby as blackmail. It was the only way. Dove's voice was pathetic as she remembered her little boy. But it was queer — even as she recalled him, she couldn't see him. Her grieving mother's voice seemed to talk him away. It was as if she'd betrayed Bobby. He was really dead now.

Travice was a man, but he was crying. Dove had won him away from the Thorns; she had made him into a child again, as he lay with his head in her lap. He said he would do anything to make up for Bobby, and Dove patted his head absently, and knew that the rest would be easy. There was no need for guilt; she made plans in her head. Other people hired men to work their land — the Thorns could do it, too. Dove and Travice were going back to Appleton: the baby would be born there.

Seven

And because of the war, providing you were nowhere near it, the world could be a cosier place. Suddenly you stopped being alone, there were so many things you could belong to. There was the Committee of Domestic Economy, the League of Loyal Women, the Patriotic Fund ... and knitting circles, sewing circles, sock clubs.

You didn't want to have a loved one fighting, of course, for there was a chance nothing could bring him back. Not even the gold kewpie charm mascot you sent, or the pocket Bible (everybody knew someone whose soldier relative had been miraculously preserved when the bullet was stopped by the Bible in his breast pocket). Why shouldn't it be you who remembered each year with the poem in the newspaper:

> *He has sailed on his last commission,*
> *In a beautiful boat called Rest;*
> *He was just an Australian hero,*
> *One of God's bravest and best.*

Their graves were always lonely, across the deep blue sea, so far from the land of the wattle; they were dear Artie, dear Jack, dear Bert who'd answered their country's call. But while they lived, before they played out their parts at Ypres and Passchendaele, you packed the Christmas box, sewed flannel undershirts, knitted socks. And joyfully tackled fly-veils for the horses in Egypt and Palestine; and saved newspapers and made

106

jam for the military hospitals. There were flag days and fêtes, bazaars and continentals, patriotic dog and cat shows. It was so pretty on Violet Day, with all the ladies in white and the scent of the violet wafting everywhere, its incense symbolizing the fragrance of lives cheerfully surrendered for duty's sake.

The war had even reached Appleton. Dove went over to the vicarage with the other ladies and they spread a big rug on the floor and sat down and started cracking almonds — they would be boxed and sent to the soldiers; and she was best in the sewing circle at making wristbands, but she was no good at socks — somehow she couldn't knit a smooth sock, the sort that wouldn't blister on the march. Though Our Boys came first, of course, a foreign fund gave a certain cachet and it might be the Help Roumania, the French Babies, the Polish Victims, the Russian Prisoners, but Dove chose the Belgian Relief. The bazaar at the vicarage was a success. The Belgian flag and colours were tastefully displayed; there were stalls and a bran pie on the verandah, the lawn was given up to the concert, while beyond the hedge refreshments were served. Dove helped on the cake stall. She was becomingly dressed in white, with a picturesque apron of red silk. When the last sponge sandwich was sold she walked with the vicar into the rose garden.

Under the arch of crimson ramblers they went and there was a confusion of flowers, roses were everywhere. They hung and tumbled; petals rippled, stems entangled. The crimson rose trembled soft as velvet under Dove's fingers and there were milky pink baby roses and some were greenish, icy in the centre, others petalled a sunburst of gold. The thick swooning scent was all about her; it was delicious walking so modestly with a man so refined. For Mr Lovibond had been to King's College, Cambridge and had a beautiful brow under silver hair brushed smooth. It didn't matter about his spectacles or the way he sometimes looked like a crocodile that was going to snap. For, despite his high scholar's forehead, his skin was crusty, scaly, and he had an ugly mouth that gripped its corners.

But his cultivated voice made the church service a thing of beauty and it was thrilling being with it alone, knowing that it talked just for her. Dove was glad she'd done her hair in the new Grecian coiffure and it was as if her answering voice walked a tightrope, for she sensed that under the polite proper words was a dizzy descent. His elbow brushed hers and she could see the church turrets poking up past the apple trees and her apron was such a burning shade of Belgian red. The green lawn glowed, trees glittered fuzzily as he squeezed her waist by the crested moss rose. It didn't matter that he had a wife, a lady just as refined as himself. The kiss came by the hybrid perpetuals.

It was perfectly innocent. In any case, Dove didn't care what he did as long as no one saw — if he stopped doing it she'd die. She needed comfort now that Travice had turned surly (why couldn't he settle down, what was wrong with driving for the jam factory?). Mr Lovibond was caring, she could tell him her troubles. Dove saw him in his study regularly; they sat on his sofa, very close. But it didn't matter what he did, they were respectable people, and he heard every word she confided. His voice was soothing in just the right places. She loved it when he said, "Commit yourself to Christ and all will be well." He was a man with a poet's soul and novel ideas. He'd erected a flagstaff near the church from which on high and holy days the Union Jack flew bravely. One hot Sunday he held evening service on the lawn. It was Epiphanytide, and Mr Lovibond kept everyone's attention by his vivid oratory. He pointed at the evening star and drove home the lessons to be learned by the manifestation of Christ to the Gentiles. Then "Sun of my soul" was sung in the dark and the congregation dispersed.

Being an Anglican was the best part of living in Appleton. If it hadn't been for Mr Lovibond, Dove didn't know what she would have done. Though she was perfectly happy, in a little white cottage with a garden bright with flowers. But it could never match up to the vicarage rose garden, and sometimes Dove looked in the mirror and surprised a peevish expression on her face (she felt more and more miserable, her life was a fret). Though she had everything she wanted. But she didn't want Travice (why couldn't he go off to the war?). Nothing was right, Appleton had changed. Mama was forgotten, Granpa's house had been pulled down, and now Dove wasn't the little girl — now she had a daughter, Clare.

"Clara" wouldn't have done, of course; "Clare" sounded properly English, and was still a way of making Mrs Arden seem true. Often she didn't; it didn't seem that anything extraordinary could ever have happened to Dove. Back in Appleton she felt a bitter-sweet sense of loss.

It was worse in spring. She thought of brides when she saw the apple blossom; the purple of the wild pea flower was the colour of her going-away dress. The Hills seemed to mock her. From a distance their cottage looked perfect; it sank into the trees like a house in a story, but inside it her life with Travice was stale. Was it all she was meant for when there were hedges of roses and freesias at the side of the road?

Travice drove for the jam factory, but he kept taking days off to go back to the farm. Mrs Thorn was supposed to be dying. Dove knew Travice blamed her for his mother's illness — perhaps as much as she blamed him for Bobby.

Nothing was sure, there was no substance in memory. Papa and Mama had gone (what proof did she have that they'd ever existed? — those stones in the cemetery could represent strangers who'd stolen their names); where Granpa's house had stood more apple trees flourished. What had become of the lilies and the oak-leafed geraniums? Where were the bell flowers, the violets and the little path? The garden had been Mama's pride and joy, but all that was left of it were the cruel spikes of the aloe she'd called Adam's Needle. Home had disappeared. The mulberry tree had fallen in the storm; strange children wandered by the creek.

Her woman's body weighed Dove down. She wanted to fall in the silvery thrash of grass; merge with the pale fire of the charlick, but her steps stayed ladylike as she kept to the road. Spring was cruel. The gloom under the lemon trees was a mysterious gipsy-green; it seemed to taunt the certainties of sewing circle, sock club, and her small flirtation with the vicar. Real life stayed somewhere else. The lemons were like hard yellow breasts. The grass was delicate, so juicy — it didn't seem it could ever turn summery bleached and dry.

•••

In the course of the war the weathercocks of the Allies' prospects had pointed all ways, and had even settled down to "stormy". Suddenly there was a magic reversal. The indication was that of triumph.

In Appleton one November evening, a crowd assembled outside the post office when the postmaster read out the official telegram of the signing of the Armistice. Loud cheers and the singing of patriotic airs showed the joy of the people. A charabanc dashed down the principal street bearing a ghostly effigy of the ex-Kaiser, crowned with a battered cauliflower. Several tin-can bands, accompanied by bugles and improvised trumpets, were soon marching the streets of the town.

The troopships· kept arriving; regularly, now, the Cheer-up ladies met the invalid soldiers' cars. The Town Hall bells rang; they were showered with flowers, fruit and chocolates. It was a time of excitement, a great reunion of hearts. Yet there was a black edge to the silver cloud. Thousands would come back; others would not.

After the Huns there was the 'flu fiend (had it come because the world was travelling too fast and encountering cosmic gases?). Some people gargled peroxide of hydrogen and rubbed it inside their nostrils; others wore masks to avoid infection. Camphor bags were sold for slipping inside one's blouse to ward off germs.

In June of 1919, a Victory Ball was held in the city. The Town Hall was hung with flags and laurel wreaths, while high up against the pillars were long palm branches. On the stage were war trophies in the shape of machine guns; draped over the organ were battle-scarred flags that various battalions had brought home with them. The General and the Colonel's wife stood on a dais, the guard of honour crossed bayonets, five military heralds blew a blast on their bugles, the orchestra struck

111

up the "Song of Australia" and down the khaki-held arch of steel the white-clad débutantes, with their soldier partners, were seen approaching. When the last curtsy was done, the programme began. There were waltzes and foxtrots and one-steps till midnight.

In July came the celebrations to mark the signing of the Peace Treaty. In Appleton a large gathering marched in procession to the Institute headed by the school drum and fife band. A little girl dressed in white butter-muslin as "Peace", and mounted on a white palfrey, was a prominent figure. After the addresses were read, the Peace medals were distributed. In the afternoon there were sports at the picnic ground; in the evening a large bonfire was lit on Appleton Hill.

There was no question that they'd been living in great and eventful times, the like of which they might never expect to see again. Those who'd passed through them would be able to tell their children, and their children's children, of the anxious and perilous years.

The war had altered everything — even Crystal was mixed up in the change. Suddenly she'd resumed correspondence. She was still in England, but she'd soon be home — but not with Mr Gerard. For the war that had taken him, had introduced Sergeant Belcher. He was "my dear Jack" and Crystal had met him when, a widow as well as a Red Cross worker, she'd visited the Military Hospital where he convalesced. Jack Belcher was a South Australian and so Crystal, as his wife, would be coming home, bringing Alice, the child of her first marriage, with her.

It was a different world. There were painted faces and cerise-salved lips; afternoon dances and dresses without sleeves. The foxtrot had superseded the tango, but now the smart set was even bored with that. The songs were new, too. Not: "Roses of Picardy" and "Fighting at the Dardanelles", but: "Harem Life" and "You Cannot Make Your Shimmy Shake on Tea".

Dove tried to remember George as he'd been before the war. She saw him mistily, his contours blurred, so she got out the photograph taken before he went overseas. He posed in a sea-grass armchair against an impossible antique landscape. His uniform had been borrowed for the occasion and the collar of his tunic didn't fit; his hare-lip nipped in plainly, because his moustache was shaved off. He was George, but not. Now, knowing he was gone for ever, his very ordinariness took on a mysterious aspect. Death had made him foreign; he was a member of another race.

Sometimes Dove wanted to give herself to Mr Lovibond like a gift; other times she chose George to receive her. Her mind felt all of a twist. The vicar's white hands were muddled with George's tanned ones. He was Travice's dead brother — if she'd had to marry a Thorn it should have been him. Here she was, a woman who bathed every day, and she must sleep beside someone who smelled of horse. Mr Lovibond's blend of odours was attractive: fine clerical cloth, fresh linen, eau de Cologne; George's smell, now he was a hero, had faded to that of the tissue paper, the camphor, that guarded his photo. But Travice spent most of his time with the jam factory's Clydesdales; they were all he seemed interested in, apart from his mother. Dove saw to it that he didn't touch Clare. The child should be a Sparks not a Thorn. It was an awful responsibility — the "wax to receive and marble to retain" notion of a child's soul and mind.

● ● ●

When she learned of Mrs Thorn's death, Dove cried because it was the right thing to do. Travice didn't show any emotion. Dove kept reading bits of Issy's letter aloud with a little catch in her voice, but he only shrugged and turned away. It was plain to see that he couldn't care less. It seemed that his visits to the farm had been merely an excuse to holiday from work. He'd been just as much a shirker as all those other young men who'd refused to follow the drum. The poster outside the recruiting booth exhorted BE A MAN, but they went on smoking cigarettes, standing thumbs in the armholes of their civilian dress in defiantly detached groups at street corners. Travice hadn't done his natural duty then, either — he was just as bad now. His mother, whose favourite he'd been, had died but he dodged every seemly display of feeling. He wouldn't even go back to the Mallee for the funeral. It was left for Dove to answer Issy's letter and send up the white lily wreath.

But perhaps he felt something. For he crept about, and appeared ashamed to look Dove in the face. It was as if he were lost to all sense of self-respect.

When Travice had first started at the factory, he'd talked of the horses to her — about the way they changed colour with sweat during the long days of summer; how in winter their eyes might be stung by the rain until they were as swollen as plums. But Dove soon stopped listening. She didn't want to know how their mouths made a smiling shape when they drank; how a feed of dandelions or thistles could set their nostrils trembling with pleasure. She scorned the time he spent gathering such delicacies. He was a fool who made little clucking noises with his tongue as he stroked their long sad faces.

Dove knew. She followed him when he went to the

114

factory early. She was a spy trailing him through the green morning world that drew back at his approach. She was his shadow as she entered the small space his body had made in the tangle of leaf and grass blade before it had time to close upon it. The sun swooped on the stink of dung and turned the blowflies' dance into a shimmer of midget rainbows. The fat white pigeons went about their busy strut and peck, even as his boots passed by them.

Dove waited until he'd entered the stable and then she crossed the yard, too. She stood at the doorway and searched for him. The draught-horse's body looked glittering, greasy in the velvet dusk of the stable. Travice stood close to it, he seemed to lean on the animal's massive strength. His arms arched up, his hands groped in its tousled mane as he leaned against the horse's side. Dove watched from the bright world of light. She heard the little crooning clicking noises that Travice made with his tongue, and the horse's answering purr. He was her enemy — a shaggy giant, stolid, yet sleek and veined and quivering in the muffled dark. Travice was Dove's husband, but he didn't love her any more, he didn't touch her; she despised him, but she would perish with loneliness. He crept from the house each morning to visit the stable. He seemed to wrestle stilly with something. It was as if he sought to sink away, to lose himself in the horse's body.

Then one morning Travice was up even earlier. When Dove woke he was gone. She came into the kitchen to find his note. It told her he would never be back. "Do not try to find me," it said and was he a seed to merge with the earth, a Father Christmas thistle to drift away on the wind? Dove stared at his message bemusedly; she didn't know what he meant — but she did. He'd done what she'd wanted him to do at last. She was alone, he'd left her — but it wasn't supposed to happen like this. It was a pretence to frighten her and somehow the horses were to blame. And his mother, too. Mrs Thorn taunted her from the grave.

Dove didn't want him, but she would bring him back. He was hers and he would stay with her until she told him to go. It was never meant to be like this. Not Dove abandoned and Travice set free without her consent. He wasn't man enough to elude her like that. He was a creeping, cowed thing and, as she set out to find him, her cheeks were burning, the anger was like joy. It was only a cruel joke — his way of hurting her, of paying her back for her game of spy. Even now he'd be with the horses; though, now, the factory at work, the stable would be different. Not a dim place of ritual, but ordinary, everyday. There'd be whistles and curses, the jangle of harnesses, the confused sound of hoofs from the yard.

And the steamy dung was in its place, the strutting pigeons in theirs, and a dog ran forward wagging its tail. But the welcome was of no account. She couldn't see Travice, and the men loading the waggons with jam for the city said they hadn't seen him either. But it was a lie. He was hiding from her in the factory. She ran inside to hunt him out.

Marmalade making was in progress, and the scores of cases of golden fruit presented a pretty picture. Everything was wonderfully clean; dust seemed rigidly excluded. The jam factory was famed for purity of manufacture and the great steam-heated preserving pans were so thoroughly scoured that their bright surfaces shone like mirrors. The factory hands' aprons and caps were a spotless snowy white and they were a fine lot of workers, several of whom had been provided with capital dwellings on the factory estate where they maintained cows, horses and poultry and lived healthy, happy lives with their families. But Dove hadn't known it would be like this — they were so mindlessly cheerful, so spick and span, but they worked like automatons. They were clockwork dolls as they handled the rich ripe fruit.

Knives flashed as the marmalade makers went on with their task. Slivers of fruit piled up, the air was thick with sticky-sweet perfume. Dove ran from the factory to Mr Lovibond.

He would rise from his desk where he worked at his sermon; he would sit her down beside him on the sofa and she would breathe in his choice blend of costly smells. The English poets, elegantly leather-bound, gold-tooled, behind lattice-paned glass; the views of Venice in their Oxford frames ... Dove knew that study so well. On the mantelpiece was the bust of Dante with its cold marble smile, the silver crucifix containing a relic of the True Cross ... She would nestle against him, and: "Cast your cares on Him who careth for you," he would murmur soothingly. He was a gentleman, silver-haired, with a sculptured profile and it didn't matter about his crusty complexion.

But he was tired of her, he didn't want her. They sat far apart on a pair of horseshoe-backed chairs, the rose-wood table between them. He listened to her with dreadful geniality. It was a tragedy she told him, but, listening, he reduced it to a farce. It was a mere tiff, he said. It didn't signify anything — why, even now Travice probably awaited her at the cottage. He was sensible, perfectly charming; he didn't look at her once. He said people were beginning to talk. It was better that she didn't come to see him. Footsteps seemed to hover outside the study door. When he rang the bell his wife came in with a tray. She was a pale woman with moles and a crinkled neck. She spoke to Dove kindly; the rings on her fingers sparkled coldly. Mrs Lovibond was a real woman, a vicar's wife; Dove was someone silly, a fluffy little kitten of a person as she sipped her claret, ladylike, and bit at her water biscuit and turned it into a crumbly crescent moon. They were both so jolly, invincible, as they waved her away.

The days passed and she waited for Travice to come home. If she didn't speak of his absence, and pretended he was just making another of his visits to the farm, it would be all right.

But they came to see her from the jam factory, and then it had to be true. She didn't know where he was — she had to admit it.

Dove became a puppet who sat quietly, resigned, while they told her what to do. *They* could be anyone, everyone. It was *they* who'd ascertained that he wasn't in the Mallee; *they* who'd announced his disappearance to the newspaper. Dove had no will of her own. All her anger had gone; her dreaming had deserted her, too. She didn't feel anything; she had no opinions, no illusions. She would do whatever they told her.

It was as if a glass dome had fallen upon her, sealing her off from an alien world. Even Clare seemed like a stranger.

The vicar came to see her. He said she must leave Appleton. It was no good staying where old memories plagued her. The cottage should be sold, he said. He knew two clergymen who needed a housekeeper.

118

Part Two
Beauville

One

They got off the tram and crossed the road, and then home for Clare was a building like a palace with balconies and loggias, spires and turrets, barley-sugar columns and a scattering of shiny gilt crosses. Its thousand windows stared past red brick and Virginia creeper to quiz her, to scorn the skimpy dress she'd outgrown, the suitcase fastened with twine. She was no one, the windows said, but she was lucky to be there, her mother told her again. Not every Protestant who applied was accepted. Tears pricked Clare's eyes as they walked up the sharp gravel path. They went past pale Jesus holding out His hands and Mary, Mother of God, in Her blue gown sprigged with stars. Far away, very faint, came the sound of children singing. The front door was beautiful, with saints' faces smiling from the stained glass panels, but her mother was going to leave her. She pressed a bell they couldn't hear ring. Now the singing had ceased. There were muffled footsteps behind the door and the saints' faces shivered. Clare was afraid, for there'd been so many moves — so many new homes — but until now they'd never been parted for long. Then the door opened and she must be brave, her mother said, as she pushed her forward towards the nun who stood there.

• • •

That first night at the orphanage, lying alone in the narrow bed, in a room full of breathing, she thought back over her life — of all the different places where they'd lived.

First there were the Hills, and Clare couldn't remember, but it meant a time when she had a father. "Travice Thorn," Mother said dreamily as she showed Clare his photo. "Your father, who died in the war." In the background was a misty land of legend; he loomed before it, sturdy in the sea-grass chair. Clare studied him, stared into his sepia eyes. It was her father. But she didn't feel anything, he stayed a stranger — yet Mother was watching her: it was Clare's duty to look mournful. His mouth was puckered, his uniform didn't fit, but dying in France had made him perfect. Mother still loved him so much that she couldn't bear to speak of him.

Moving from the Hills had been a mistake. They could have stayed at the cottage — Mother was a good cook, there were a number of bachelors in the town, she might have taken in boarders. But the vicar suggested the move, and it was the beginning of always living with others. The two clergymen were kind; their surplices billowed, latticed with lace, to make a pleasant memory in Clare's head. But Mother heard of the position at the seaside hotel, and so they moved on.

She worked there for a while, and then had a little shop next to it where she made pies and pasties and did morning teas and oyster suppers. Clare watched her wade into the sea in front of the hotel to get the oysters. It was a town of sandy streets and shabby weatherboard houses sheltered by coprosma hedges and dusty geraniums. Holiday-makers licked penny ice-creams as they strolled past the fish shop's mysterious notice that said: SNAPPER SQUID SNOOK. Anglers knelt on the beach to hunt seaworms for bait; there were rocks pelted with seaweed, a cliff carpeted with midget pussy-tails. Remembering, the time they spent there seemed always summery. Clare recalled setting suns that drew wonderful mosaics on the waters and transformed the limbs of bathers into splendid models of burnished copper. The paddles of a canoe flashed goldenly as it glided past; the white whiskers of an old man carrying a fishing bag and rod were put back to the ruddy tints of youth. At night, merging and mingling with the roar of the ocean, the sighing of the wind, came the sound of pianos, the twanging of a banjo, voices singing "Look for the Silver Lining" ...

They might have stayed for ever, but her mother was restless. She couldn't settle down. The perfect place was always somewhere ahead.

Next, Mother worked for wealthy people in the city but she wasn't allowed to have Clare with her. So when the retired schoolmistress advertised for a child to look after for company it seemed just the thing. Her house in the country was cosy, she was kind enough, but Clare fell ill with pneumonia. When Mother came she recovered, but as soon as she left Clare had a relapse. She was fretting, so the schoolmistress sent for her mother again, and Clare was wrapped in a rug and went down to the city on the coach, and was smuggled into the servants' quarters. It was a big house with a big kitchen and Clare had to be quiet. In the end she was found out and so her mother left to keep house for an old lady. They were with her for nearly two years, then took a room in a boarding-house, for now Mother had found work at another hotel. It was then that things started to go wrong for Clare. Till then, they'd still been carting round their own furniture — they slept side by side in the brass bed that had come from the cottage in the Hills. But now the furniture was sold, and it felt queer to sleep separate in single beds. And Mother was needed to help with evening dinner — Clare hated the loneliness of night-time. She used to buy little penny fairy-stories and sit on the doorstep and read them. Mother was too busy, and Clare was neglected. She was always alone. Then someone told her mother about the orphanage.

Eventually, that first night, Clare fell asleep to dream of the happy time they'd spent by the sea. It seemed so real — Mother hitched up her skirt and her legs gleamed pinkly as she waded towards the oyster bed. The turquoise sea leaped and curled, then dashed in — milky, curdled — to make small wavelets and little foaming eddies, while above the spangled spray, a ghostly sea mist floated in, too. The dream was all silvery, shimmering with light, as Clare held Mother's hand and waded with her towards the sand. But then the great rocks loomed up like crouching animals. The wetted weed that grew on them made them look furred; they crouched snug, yet menacing, like wet fur coats. And then Mother's hand was gone, and Clare was awake. The dormitory was still dark; she was surrounded by the breathing of strangers and her life seemed miserable. She thought of all those past nights when her mother had cried quietly and she'd lain beside her in the brass bed, pretending sleep — wondering what was wrong, knowing it was the fact of her father's dying. Mother sobbed on, so gently, effortlessly, that she might have been laughing softly. Clare stayed calm, uncaring. Every other girl in the world might have a father, but she didn't mind being left out. She was glad he'd died. Because he had, Mother was hers, she didn't have to share her.

Clare had loved her mother jealously, but she'd paid her back for her devotion by doing this: banishing her to a place where nuns glided like queer black swans, and every other girl had knelt to mutter prayers, and the strange bed felt like a coffin. Clare hated Mother for being so cruel, and went on remembering the bad times ... not the spoonful of condensed milk she was allowed as a treat, but that time she ate the Condy's crystals and it made her tongue purple and tasted horrid and Clare was crying and trying to wash it off when Mother came home. She was angry and said: "You might die." That night had been as awful as this early morning — Clare had lain awake all through it, afraid.

But life went on. In some ways it was easier. All the orphanage children were fatherless; most lacked a mother, too. Clare felt herself turn anonymous, it was oddly comforting. There was no one, now, to jeer at her dowdy clothes, for the orphanage children were dressed alike. Though it was strange to be labelled with a number — Clare's was 48, and it was printed inside her pinafore.

They went to Mass every morning. Clare was always late, she was always forgetting her hat and it was terrible to go into Mass without one. She had to gather up her pinafore at the back and drape it over her head like a veil. On Sundays the pinafores were special, with a frill over each shoulder, and they went out of the orphanage gates and down the road in a crocodile to the church. There were boys at the orphanage, too, but they were in another wing so the girls hardly saw them — Sunday church was the only regular time.

Bath night, when they bathed two at a time — one at each end of the bath — meant they must wear a calico overall in the water. Clare hated having to take her clothes off and put on the uninviting wet garment passed down from the bather before her.

She grew used to sleeping in the long cold dormitory, and walking down the zigzag iron staircase to the schoolroom and the refectory. The meals were shocking. There was boiled sausage and a bit of mince; bread and a scrape of plum jam. Another bad thing was that the other girls had nightdresses, but Clare had pyjamas. The problem was to get into them without anyone seeing a part of her body. She went through the worry nightly, for immodesty was a sin.

Other girls lived lives that were different. The chilly winds of the world were kept at bay by a warm clasp of hands. Mother and Father, Granma and Granpa, Aunt and Uncle — the golden girls were protected by a snug bolster of family, all the chinks that let in loneliness were stopped up. They walked out secure, accompanied by legends and memories that enshrined a host of relatives for ever larger than life. They knew who they were, family-trees spread their generations before them. God, for those girls, would be a genial Santa; Death merely signify a happy-ever-after Heaven.

Clare had only Mother. In the old days they'd slept together. Sometimes Clare had fitted her body about Mother's, and they'd been two spoons lying in a silk-lined cutlery box — it had felt so cosy, so perfectly safe. If Clare woke from a nightmare, Mother's body had been there, breathing and warm, to cling to for courage.

Separated from Mother, Clare's life seemed sad; all its gipsying something to regret. In the orphanage, where to be fatherless and motherless and homeless was commonplace, the fantasy of a family and a fixed home was the thing that was constantly yearned for. Ordinariness was what counted. An orphan drew status from the living not the dead, from the relatives in the world she could claim. Clare had a mother, she should have felt secure; but she didn't know anything about her mother's past, except that she'd come from the Hills and married a man who'd died. Mother's solitariness only underlined Clare's own condition.

Clare was encompassed by a mystery. Sometimes its nebulous mists turned solid, and it was like being immured in the wall of a dungeon. When her mind moved it seemed to bump against stone — Clare thought about her aloneness so often that it hurt. Who was she, why was she here? What was her mother's story; who had her father been? Her child's mind couldn't tell her, a dead hero in a photograph was no help. Mother was cruel. She refused to talk of her past in the Hills. She didn't speak of her parents; she never mentioned brothers or sisters.

TWO

Something called The Board was expected. Because of it, the orphanage was transformed. Floors had been made perilous with beeswax, incense sickened the air. Corridors were looped with evergreen garlands; the comforting gloom had been swept away from countless images of Jesus to reveal hearts like pincushions spilling teardrops of blood. In the Mother Superior's parlour the pieces of bone from St Peter and St Paul were displayed in their silver reliquary on the mantelpiece beside a vase of lady's slipper, lady's thimble, lady's thumb — all flowers named in honour of the Virgin.

The cupboard in the dormitory where the special pinafores were kept came open. It wasn't Sunday, but every girl must put hers on. Then they must stand in a line while Sister Moira flapped past inspecting. She looked more sinister than usual. The pebble-lenses of her spectacles had been polished to a blinding brilliance; her whimple whispered scratchily, her habit was shifty with shadows.

She was the nun who always held her rosary beads when she walked so they wouldn't hear her coming. She made them look at the picture of the Five Holy Wounds; she told about St George on his wheel of spikes. This morning she inspected every particle of skin that showed. Any girl with nettle rash, morbid sweat, or itch was marched away. Everyone else must be a model orphan in the schoolroom.

Clare was almost eight years old — she could read and write, but was constantly baffled by her sums. This day was no exception. After Sister Moira reminded them of the girl who chewed the nut on her way to First Communion (it was a mortal sin, so she died) they started on long division. Clare's page was soon covered with crosses and she was strapped on the legs and stood out the front on a form. She was so ashamed that she couldn't stand upright. She stood bent over like a little old woman. Then Sister Moira saw she was wearing the corals. At the same time The Board came in.

Suddenly the room was full of ladies with dead foxes round their necks and gentlemen with glinting watch-chains. But Clare was an example: the punishment must go on. There was a terrible silence, for the sin was compounded. She couldn't do arithmetic and the corals meant vanity. It had been bad enough when one of the big girls had worn the ring with the chip of diamond, but this was far worse: Clare was a little girl and a ring disgraced a mere finger, while the corals encircled her wrist.

But it was really a necklace, and once it had been Mother's. When she'd been a baby she'd worn it, but one birthday she'd given it to Clare. It was the prettiest thing she had, her only keepsake from home. Usually it stayed wound round her arm, tucked away from sight beneath her sleeve. Somehow it had slipped down to give her away. And now she couldn't get it off. Her fingers were all thumbs as she fumbled in vain. Sister Moira's stick came down on her knuckles and then her nun's fingers were clawing at the corals, tearing at Clare's wrist. There was a sound like a sigh as the cord they were strung on to broke; then a sharp sound, surprising, as coral beads peppered the floor.

While it happened, the strange faces stared down at her. She was circled by avid purple mouths and nipped-in pale ones, chins that nestled on pearls large as pigeons' eggs, eyes wobbling glassily on a pouched nest of lines; and there were slivers of pink tongue, nostrils strung with hair; and angry black shave-dots, caterpillar moustaches, beards resembling miniature hooked rugs.

But one gentleman member of the Orphanage Board was clean-shaven. His peach-bloom face was young, but he dressed in an old-fashioned way. The other gentlemen members were modern with bulldog toes, torpedo-shaped cuff-links and dog's-tooth check trousers; their ties were gaily patterned with school and club and regimental colours in diagonal stripes. But his clothes were sober and mostly black. He wore a crape armband on the sleeve of his frock coat; he carried a highly polished silk hat and an ebony stick. As the beads bounced over the schoolroom floor he stooped to gather them up.

After the last coral went into his pocket, instead of following the others down the aisles to inspect scholastic achievement, he lingered before Clare, leaning on his stick, scrutinizing her closely. He peered and peered at her; walking round her to view from all angles, as if he were a collector and she an object he contemplated possessing. At last he nodded his head, seemingly satisfied with what he saw. Clare didn't feel indignant at his appraisal. Because of it, she was someone important. The other girls looked at her curiously, while Sister Moira glared her displeasure.

Clare felt quiet, at peace. She didn't care about losing her corals — she was glad he had them in his pocket; she felt almost as if they belonged there. Sister Moira, and the rows of girls dipping their pens rhythmically into inkwells disappeared; nothing seemed to exist except Clare and the gentleman. It was as if they stood linked together, cut off from everything commonplace, in a sealed world of their own.

He began asking her questions. His voice was soothing, it sounded like music. He was dark — very dark; he wore his curly hair so long that he might have been an actor; he was such a small man that Clare, standing on her form, was nearly as tall as he. He was quite the nicest person she'd encountered. He listened intently to all she said. It didn't seem that he was a stranger. She might have known him all her life.

When she told him her name, it pleased him. "Clare, Clare ..." he repeated softly, as though savouring the flavour of its sound. Then his velvety voice played a game with her name. "Clara, Clara ... " he murmured, turning it foreign. He liked the "Dove" that was her mother's name, too; her father's "Travice", also.

But when he asked Clare if her father had ever been found, she didn't know what he meant. He'd made a mistake, she said, for her father hadn't wandered away. Instead, Travice Thorn had been killed in the war. The fact was the only sure thing in Clare's life. While everything kept changing, as home kept being in different places, the finality of his hero's death was comforting. Clare mightn't feel anything when she looked at his photograph, but his dying placed her — and her mother, too. His death gave their lives meaning.

Until now, Clare had never spoken of it to anyone. But his dark eyes gazed at her so steadily. It was wonderful. He was a gentleman of rare distinction with a Piccadilly collar, a puffed Ascot, a coat of best vicuna — and she interested him, he wanted to know all about her.

Clare waited for something to happen. Somehow, after meeting him, she knew her life would change.

It wasn't a surprise when she was summoned to the Mother Superior's parlour. But she hadn't imagined the motor car or the chauffeur with his cap. And his pants flared out above his click-heeled boots, and he held the door open as if she counted. It wasn't a joke, though the little winged lady on the bonnet winked silverly.

From the outside, the orphanage still resembled a palace, but inside, the Board's visit over, the garlands had been taken down, the incense had floated away. The Jesuses would get dusty and turn trickily comforting again: the orphans would forget about the horrid bleeding hearts. But now they still remembered, and from the windows they watched Clare depart. They looked ugly with their noses pressed against the pane. Not one of them was smiling because they envied her so much.

People stared as the glittering car went by. Clare pitied them, walking out in an everyday world, while she sat back on dimpled leather. It was the dream car with a silver flower vase, ash-trays, silk blinds.

They drove through streets where the leaves of the hedges were as shiny as patent leather and wistaria petalled the footpath. Tudor gables rose up, lace curtains billowed gently; there was a Sunday feeling with pianos playing and sleek-faced ladies taking puppies for walks. Then the streets narrowed and the stately houses were replaced by little blunt ones that hid their verandahs behind striped canvas blinds.

The people and the houses and the streets grew

shabbier. For a while they drove beside a railway line and the landscape was as bleak as a battlefield, there was a melancholy smell of ashes. Then the road was a big one with traffic everywhere, and shops took the place of houses. All the people hurried, but the car raced past them and soon everything was different again. Now it was like the country. The road was a dirt one twisting between paddocks, and a woman flung wheat and roosters ran about. Clare saw spotted cows, vegetables in rows beside a river ... and then it might have been a dream, for there were Chinamen as well as watermelons.

The car sped over a plank bridge towards the swampy reedbeds of the river's further bank. Then they were enclosed by a wilderness of willows and gum trees, and the road petered out before a pair of iron gates set in a stone wall. From the reeds came a terrible shrieking, a wild clapping of wings, as birds flew into the sky.

The gates led into an old-world garden. Clare saw formal flower beds, primly-cut hedges, trees clipped to geometric proportions. There was a sundial, marble statues, and on the still lake's surface floated water lilies, white swans. It was a picture-book place, so green and serenely calm, but none of the birds could fly. For, as the car slowly approached the house, great speckled creatures — the fattest birds Clare had ever seen — made startled waddles across the drive. First one, then another, would leap at the air, but every ungainly try at flight only ended in a clumsier tumble to earth. It seemed that behind the wall all the birds' wings had been clipped, even those of the peacocks that strutted about the old lady on the verandah.

Arden House reminded Clare of the orphanage. It was built of similar red brick and was covered with the same sort of creeper that, as it fluttered, gave the house the appearance of breathing. But the lady on the verandah was worse than a nun. Her pale skin was so wrinkled that she must be a hundred years old, though she stood stiff and straight in her ancient gown. Her old fingers felt cold as they gripped Clare's hand. The bunch of keys that hung from her belt jingled angrily as she led her into the house.

It was a handsome drawing-room, with its black wallpaper powdered over with gold sunflowers; its black carpet set about with an assortment of sofas and sociables, footstools and chairs, luxuriously padded and fringed and tasselled in gold satin and velvet and silk. And there were occasional tables, whatnots, cabinets; and spindly gilt chairs, a stately gilt harp, large mirrors in elaborate gilt frames. The deep gold curtains were drawn though it was day, and the room was lit by clusters of wax candles. All manner of rich and curious objects were scattered about, to gleam dully in the subdued light. Over the black marble fireplace was a life-size portrait in oils of an old lady and a little boy.

The old lady stood there darkly, looking out at the black and gold room. She was so real. Clare could see the net of veins on her hand, the shadow like a scab beneath her full pouting lip. Her face was alarmingly fat; she smiled smugly, sweetly, as if her mouth were stuffed with chocolate creams. She made Clare think of jellies, queen cakes, currant buns. She was a pink-frosted biscuit of an old lady, with a sugar scroll of a mouth and slippery eyes. But she was also a great black bird — her sooty dress was fluttery with veils, glittery with a queer collection of ornaments: beads like sparkly dead ants, lockets in the shape of midget coffins; a variety of sombre brooches and pins and buttons. The old lady was smiling, but she was also crying into a black-bordered hanky.

The child on a cushion at her feet was a perfect little fellow, rosy-cheeked, with fine dark eyes and shiny curls. The sort of child who would have been lapped round from birth with the safe sure love that an orphan dreamed of. And he never had to share his bath, and the water would be warm and soapy, he could show as much of his body as he pleased; and breakfast would be eggs and bacon, toast fingers, jam. He was so pampered and pretty; such a small cavalier in his old-fashioned suit. He gazed fondly up at the old lady and nestled close to her bunchy skirts — she must have loved him dearly; the life they'd lived together, off the canvas, must have been good. Clare moved closer to the mantel-piece and gazed up — over the elegant clock, the ivory statuette, the lustres with their dangling crystal drops ... and suddenly she knew who he was. His child's face wasn't so different from his adult one. The picture boy had grown up to be Mr Arden, the gentleman who'd pocketed Clare's corals and had gone on to have her brought from the orphanage to this splendid room in his house.

They entered the room so quietly that they took her by surprise. Clare left off studying Mr Arden as a child to see him standing before her, grown up.

The smaller of the two women with him stood there stilly, like a figure in a frieze. Her tailored coat and skirt were a demure pearly grey; she wore a matching hat trimmed with silver leaves. Her face was bowed down. As she lifted her head, Clare saw that it was Mother.

But Mother's hair had been long and it went up on her head, puffed out with the false bits, held in place with side combs and pins. The pins used to fall out and she'd use them to hunt wax in her ears. But now she was perfect. Her hair was cut short and set in marcel-waves; she had pearls round her neck and drop ear-rings. She was charming and elegant. But she looked terrible. Under the powder there were little twitching lines and she was as skinny as a leaf, and Clare didn't care what magic had brought her here — she didn't care as Mr Arden said that Mother had been ill and wasn't it lucky that he'd been able to find her. Even Mother's fingernails were painted and her smell was different and Clare hated her — she wanted the old Mother, the old days, and being ill could never make up for her sending Clare to the orphanage. But Mr Arden said she had to — so she went into the painted lady's arms and it must look a pretty picture, with them reunited, but Clare knew that Mother didn't want her. She stayed stiff and far away inside her new clothes; she was a body embalmed, with a new face, and the only thing that was real about her were her hands. They grew out of her sharp nails all red and ugly, they were the same hands that used to smell of fish and onions and washday, but now they smelled flowery of hand cream. Clare pushed Mother's hands away and she didn't care but "Stop that crying," said the other woman, the big one with Mother and Mr Arden. But why wasn't it Mother's voice, caring enough to be angry, why was the old wrinkled lady leading her from the room?

Clare was quiet now, but the big woman said to pull herself together. And she said it was plain that the child had her mother's nerves, and she'd been spoiled, and it was the fault of being with Catholics and they could do anything then go and confess and start all over again. She was big with a red face and smouldering eyes. Her mouth was sulky beneath its feminine moustache. There was a suppressed rage in the regular rise and fall of her dark serge bodice, peppered over with little bright beads. Yet there was an air of denial and disappointment about her. She was a gloomy sort of woman, unstylish, despite her bonfire looks. She was Aunt Rosa, Mother's long-lost sister.

Mr Arden had another surprise. Mother had come to live at Arden House; she would be a help to his housekeeper, Rudd. But it was a lonely house, no place for a child. But Clare would never go back to the orphanage. Mr Arden had it all arranged. Clare would live with Aunt Rosa and Uncle Will in the house beside their bakery at Beauville.

Three

The move to Beauville had been a tragedy for Rosa. She hated people knowing she lived there. Though, because the Port Road cut the suburb in two, she could be thankful that she lived on the right side. The river and its factories stayed across the road. The Priddles' part of Beauville meant a row of little streets: First Street, Second Street, Third ... all the way on down to Fifteenth, and a gasometer and a railway line and a disused pughole, but it was also bordered by a road that climbed up to the golf-links and the parklands and the flash houses where rich people lived. Because of that road and its dizzy ascent, Rosa took heart and said she lived at Beauville-on-the-Hill.

And she had to admit, grudgingly, that the house — though shabby and lacking amenities — was all right. There was an upstairs and the rooms were huge, and along one side was a glassed-in conservatory. Rosa was fond of plants and filled it with fuchsias and fern baskets and wax flowers in pots.

And, really, despite being common, the majority of Beauville people appeared respectable. They didn't empty their slops if a neighbour was about; they knew their place, and gave their orders humbly when Rosa served in the shop. A councillor lived on Priddles' side of the street, so there was kerbing, though it stopped abruptly after his house.

Even in Beauville verandahs were regularly polished,

lace curtains starched, and gravel raked. Sometimes Rosa felt sentimental — it seemed a sort of happy poverty that she'd sunk to. Though she would never forgive Peggy for turning Salvationist, and singing outside the Gasworks Hotel on Friday nights. Peggy took after her father and, thinking about it, Rosa grew angry again. Then she thought of Ralph, and was comforted. Ralph had her longing for better things; he practised the art of sugar-work determinedly. It was tragic that he should be out delivering with his weak heart. He was an artist, meant for more than penny buns and bread.

One night Rosa dreamed that she was driving with Papa in the buggy. She was a girl again. She sat close to him, she leaned against his black shoulder. He wore his gentleman's clothes and she was safe. But suddenly they'd left the quiet Hills behind. In the dream, now, the din of the traffic was terrible. Horns blew, and motor cars rumbled. Strange horses screamed and bared crooked teeth as whips came down on their backs. They pulled carts heaped with bleeding rabbits and rusty iron, and the buses were covered with advertisements for cough cures and boot polish. It was the Port Road, and Rosa was afraid, and the closer she pressed against Papa for comfort, the more he shrank away — until he was just a humped black overcoat, until he wasn't there at all. Now Rosa rode in the buggy alone, and the pawn shop was crammed with false teeth and wedding-rings; the pig's head in the butcher's shop leered. It was Beauville — a ghastly place, all poverty and struggle, where people were sleepwalkers, though they surged over the pavement in swarms: old people with walking-sticks and dust in their hat brims, women who clutched their coats as if they had bellyaches, ragged men with matted beards, boys with dangerous eyes, girls with blistered lips ...

Next morning the house was hideous. She saw the cracks in the walls, the ancient ingrained grime that no amount of scrubbing could remove. She kept thinking of Betsy Dew who lived next door and had her boy friends in for love sessions. The sky outside the window was a sickly grey, a nasty smell had got into everything and Rosa was old and Papa was dead.

Years ago there'd been heroes, giants in black coats, and each day was an adventure. Rosa met Will Priddle at a party where she wore her new white dress and there was a swing hanging from a walnut tree and the boys swung the girls and Will swung her that night and walked her home and it meant she was his sweetheart. They did their courting at church and paid a penny and signed the pledge — lemonade was their drink, and how could she have guessed that he won her by false pretences, that it would turn out the way it did? For even when he wore the temperance badge he went down to the pub on the sly, and it just turned from bad to worse. But in the beginning they ate little tart summer strawberry apples, and there was a tree with white flowers like snow wreaths and Rosa linked Will's arm and breathed in spicy garden scents. Then, it seemed that Will would be as much of an adventurer as Papa. He was going to take her away to the city and their life would be wonderful. Will would have a bakery of his own and to begin with they'd live modestly, but in no time there'd be a fleet of bakery carts and PRIDDLE seen everywhere in large gold letters. But Rosa missed out, the good times never came to stay, and at the parties there'd been a game where everyone stood tight together in the passage in a line and when it was "Go" they pushed back, and it happened once that Rosa was last in the line and she took the full force of the push and felt queer, and it was

140

how she felt all the time now — queer, permanently winded.

But then Mr Arden called. Rosa opened the door to a chance at a different life. The street had never seen a car like his before, and the neighbours were peeping from behind their curtains as she asked him in. He brought back the old days. He'd been just a child then — but he remembered Papa fondly. Ebenezer Sparks came alive again as they sat at the kitchen table, and its oilcloth surface was sordid, Rosa had never regretted the loss of her elegant furniture more. She'd had to sell everything, and Valentine Arden knew how she felt, he sympathized, and went on to make his proposal. She bridled up a bit when he first mentioned Dove, and his voice went smoother, softer, but she heard every word, for money was in his voice now. It wouldn't be as if the child's coming would put them out of pocket, quite the reverse, but it would mean condoning the lie of Travice's death — but his voice was persuasive. It was for Ralph's sake that Rosa agreed. He would decorate the cakes he'd always dreamed of, and the élite would leave their mansions and come down the hill to purchase Priddles' afternoon tea fancies. Valentine was sure of it, he said the bakery being in Beauville would add a novel touch.

Mr Arden sent Clare some new clothes. Aunt Rosa held them up one by one, and said she'd never seen such beautiful dresses. She was the child, not Clare, as she traced the pattern of lace insertion with a washday-rough finger; as she stroked Fuji silk frills and flounces, and wondered over puffed organdie sleeves and skirts that stood out like little crinolines. Auntie said she'd never seen anything like it: the frock of black velveteen, the velour coat with the fur collar; the princess under-skirts, the embroidered bloomers; the ribbed cashmere socks, the patent ankle-strap shoes. Even the school tunic was of finest navy twill, the white Tobralco blouse was finished with pearl buttons.

Aunt Rosa came out of her dream. It wasn't bath night, but she had to light the copper and sigh awfully each time she poured a bucket of boiling water into the bath-tub. Then the cold went in, and then Clare. It should have been a treat (on bath night Peggy had used the water first, and Clare always washed in a hurry because there was the feeling that Ralph was watching), but Clare couldn't forget the fact that the bath meant another visit to Arden House.

And yet Clare missed Mother more and more. So much time had passed, that the pain of their encounter in the black and gold room had stopped hurting. The painted lady with the uncaring smile who cut off her hair and went to live with Mr Arden didn't seem true. Clare's mother had a body that was soft and real ... when she came to bed her face was different. She'd rubbed away her rosy cheeks; wiped off her painted smile. Clare was supposed to shut her eyes while Mother undressed — usually she did, but sometimes she saw Mother's body, pink as a sea-shell in the candlelight ...

As Clare put on the new silk dress, she felt better. Peggy left off serving in the shop to inspect her, and she reckoned that Clare looked just like Dove. Then the car was there and they took the same route as last time — soon it was like the country, with market-gardens and Chinamen. They crossed the bridge and birds flew out of the reeds; behind the wall that enclosed Arden House, other birds scuttled helplessly.

Mr Arden was waiting for her in the drawing-room. But when she'd seen him last, and that first time at the orphanage, he'd seemed like her friend. Now he was cold and distant. She had to stand still while he walked round her — he'd done the same thing at the orphanage, but then Clare had felt important. Now, as he considered whether the new dress suited or not, she felt worthless. The gilt harp and the sofa covered in old-gold velvet were perfect, but his judging eyes told her she was flawed. And then his mouth went as sneering as a camel's and he rang the bell for Rudd. When she came, he told her that something must be done about the child's hair. Its smell was so bad that he couldn't bear to have her near him.

Clare was swept away down a long draughty passage to a bathroom, chill and marbly as a mausoleum, and she saw gold taps shaped like fish and rainbow shells in a glass bowl, and then she was shrouded in a towel and it was the worst humiliation yet. Rudd's bony fingers were moving over her head — and it had happened to other girls at the orphanage: the careful inspection, then eucalyptus oil rubbed in — and she grunted happily whenever Clare winced as the fine-tooth comb raked her scalp.

After her hair was washed, Clare walked in the garden. The swans glided on the lake; the velvety lawns were edged with bright flower beds; round the sundial was carved:

> Let others tell of storms and showers,
> I'll only tell your sunny hours.

But it was a stiff glaring place, as tidy as a public park, and perhaps she'd see REMEMBER THE ANZACS spelled out in pansies. All the flowers, and even the chocolate earth, looked expensive. The garden was as tame as a florist's display. The simple-faced flowers were circled by snail killer; there wasn't a weed in sight.

Then she went down a flight of mossy steps, and branches were all about her. The great tree bent so low that it made a silky tent of leaves. Beyond it, weeds tangled everywhere: the garden had turned wild.

Thistles cast their parachutes of snowy hairs; there were ragged flowers running to seed, a host of wiry creeping stems. No one could mind her being there, but she felt like a trespasser. It was such a private wilderness, so secret and hidden. And then she was surrounded by a nightmare company of staring ghosts. But they were only statues — a boy grimaced as he plucked at the thorn in his foot, cherubs puffed out their cheeks.

On the lawn a peacock shook himself and spread his spangled tail, then swung round to show off another lesser tail — modestly grey, and the black powderpuff of feathers beneath it. As Clare walked back towards the house she looked up, and saw a figure standing at one of the attic windows. Creeper groped at the pane, but Mother stood there stiff and still. Her face was fixed and white, and then it faded away. Rudd was waiting on the verandah. As Clare followed her into the house, the peacock threw back its crested head and gave out a series of dismal screams.

Mother called her name so merrily as she entered the room. She scooped Clare up and hugged her. Her cheeks were rosy as carnations, she'd never looked lovelier, but she was a lady playing a role. Her shot silk blouse changed its colour every time she moved. She was all twitchy, her voice was fluttering. Mr Arden watched every movement, he listened for every word.

For a moment Mother hung her head low and then, as if she sensed Mr Arden's displeasure, she lifted her chin and smiled. She was like a tame petted animal, a canary bird singing mindlessly, and fear was in her turtle-dove eyes. Mr Arden stood behind her, his hand rested lightly on her shoulder. She stiffened as his hand caressed her white neck.

Don't forget me, said Mother's eyes. Don't remember me as I am now, but when I was the Mother who lived at the sea and slept against you in the brass bed. And I sang "Peg O' My Heart" when you woke early and gave you butterfly kisses. And remember when I chased you with the strap, when I spilled hot fat on your leg by mistake and burned your chest with the mustard plaster. I was real then.

Four

Clare's cousin, Peggy Priddle, was eighteen but she seemed like a little girl. It was because she'd been sick as a child. She'd had shocking headaches, and never had to fall in at school because if she stood up too long she'd faint. The other girls called her Teacher's Pet but she couldn't help it. She'd been so thin that her mother used to call her in off the street so people wouldn't see her. One day her hair went white because she had infected teeth. So when she was twelve she had to go to Mr Blitz, the dentist, and have one tooth out a week. Most people only had two sets of natural teeth, but Peggy had three — her third lot was in her gums, all pressed up. They came down after she had the second lot out, and her hair went back to its colour and the headaches stopped and she started growing.

But at school they still called her Skinny Mick and she used to cry. But her father said you never saw a fat racehorse, you couldn't fatten a thoroughbred.

Peggy had a monkey face and a stoop in her back, but her hair was lovely. It was midnight black and so long that she could sit on it. She did hair drill every night, rubbed in coconut oil with her fingertips and brushed and brushed. So she wouldn't have a snow-storm in summer, she used Ayer's Hair Vigor that melted the flakes of dandruff away.

During the war Peggy knitted socks for the soldiers. She used to do the plain and pearl on the top, and then her mother would do the leg part — the plain — because she couldn't do pearl, and then Peggy would do the heel, and then her mother would go on and do up to the toe, which would be left for Peggy to finish. Peggy reckoned she'd knitted more socks as a child than anyone else. She used to put notes to the soldiers in the toes, but she never ever got a reply.

Peggy was glad that Clare had come to live in the house at Beauville. It was cosy to share her bedroom with her cousin. Before Clare came, Peggy would wake up and be scared by queer shapes in the dark.

Peggy was in the Salvation Army. She mustn't cut her hair, and all ornamental ways of dressing it, such as frizzings, fringes, or tufts were forbidden. When Peggy delivered the *War Cry* and sang under the banner inscribed with "Blood and Fire", and did knee drill and attended Salvation Meeting, she had her hair wound round her head under her hallelujah bonnet in a prim snake of plait. But at night in her bedroom, with just Clare to see, she experimented with pompadours and Psyche knots and turban coiffures.

Dancing had no place in a Salvationist's life, but in the bedroom Peggy practised the circular waltz, partnered by a chair, until she got dizzy going round and round. And she saved the Paou Chung tea packets. Not because of the picture of the pagoda or the mysterious Chinese hieroglyphics, but on account of the packet being red. She'd dip it in water and rub it on her mouth and cheeks.

Because Peggy was liable to have colds in the head, she slept in a flannel cap covering the forehead. And she had a weak chest, so she wore a rabbit-skin bib and a camphor bag under her flannel singlet. And she always took a shawl to bed with her, because babies came from

147

heaven and if God sent one he'd give it to Peggy, because she had the shawl to wrap it in.

Peggy liked to talk herself to sleep. She told the same stories over and over again. About joining the Army — how it happened when they had their open-air, and she'd followed the band back to the barracks and sat in the front row with her mouth open because she was used to being quiet in church and thought all the *Amens* and *Hallelujahs* terrible. But in the end, even though Mother didn't want her to, she joined up and first she was a Sunbeam and then a Guard and last year she got her uniform and bought the bonnet from an Army lady who was ill and wasn't going to get better. And how she had the flannelette napkins and the belt with the little calico tags to pin them to all ready, but it wouldn't come and the doctor put her in a chair with her legs apart and she had a big sheet over her and he examined her and she was terrified and he said it meant an operation to have something taken away from her brain and put somewhere else, but the next week it came and it meant she was a woman — it must have been the fright ...

Ralph was a fat young man of twenty-seven with a bald head. Clare thought he seemed a bit not all there; he didn't seem bright. He was horrible. He looked at Clare strangely, his eyes went small as seeds. He chased her with a mouse that was caught in a trap, till Uncle Will made him stop.

But he was Aunt Rosa's favourite. In her eyes he'd never grown up. She was always remembering him as a baby ... He had such pink cheeks. He had skin like wax. He got his head stuck through the bars of his cot.

Ralph used to deliver the bread. He drove round Beauville in a high two-wheeler cart with a canvas top, and went from house to house with his basket of loaves. Sometimes the horse was Old Grey, other times Molly. Old Grey had a loose stomach that went *cloop-clop, cloop-clop*. Molly had been a racehorse. She didn't like Ralph, because at one stage he hit her. Every time he went near her, she'd try to kick him.

When Ralph had finished his round, he practised decorating. Icing sugar was too dear to use, so he learned by practising with dripping. He beat it to a cream and piped through a greaseproof paper bag on to a sheet of newspaper. He could pipe curls and leaves and scrolls. Ralph reckoned it wouldn't be long before he was good enough to have a try at a wedding-cake with coconut icing, then royal icing, then sprays and silver leaves and corner pieces.

Peggy and Aunt Rosa spoke with refined voices when they served in the shop. As well as selling bread and cake they did lunches for the bottle works and the brewery.

Auntie had a way with bread, she served it up at every meal. Bread made mock turkey, mock duck, mock goose. There was bread soup, bread omelette, bread pudding, bread pancake; jelly bread, crumb-drop biscuits, breadcrumb pie. The list of dishes was endless. Bread was the staff of life and it meant disaster if you trod on a crumb.

The smell in the bakehouse was always beautiful, but Uncle had it very hard. He used to start round five o'clock in the morning and finish round noon. He made the dough the night before. When he'd mixed it in the wooden trough he'd start bashing it and sometimes the little Doody boys would come in and he'd throw some clean bags over the dough and they'd jump on it and knock it down, to save him punching it. Sometimes while he waited for it to rise, he'd sleep in the flour room on a pile of sacks. At five o'clock he'd knock the dough up and shape it into loaves and put them in the tins.

The big brick oven had to be fired up with stringy-bark for every batch of bread, and after each firing Uncle cleaned it out — scuffled out the ashes with a chaff bag on the end of a stick. He used to make his own yeast from potatoes and flour and hops. The potatoes were boiled in an iron cooking pot, and when they were done Uncle would cut one open for Clare, and she'd eat it sprinkled with salt. And she used to try out the dried fruits — take a handful at a time from each of the wooden boxes under the long table. But the best thing of all was the cream that was made of sugar and butter. Clare could have eaten it all day, but she worried she'd be sick. And there was the lovely smell of the bread and she was proud that she knew the names of the loaves: pipe loaf with its corrugations, tin loaf that didn't have much crust, the cottage loaf that was like a bun on top of a lady's head. And there was Smut, the bakery cat who kept down the mice and always snatched a scone from the first batch that came out of the oven.

Uncle was a small man, with the same sad monkey face as Peggy. But he was funny. He could make shadow animals on the wall with his fingers; he had the *Ha! Ha! Ha!* joke book. He was never too busy to tell Clare a story. About the time when Peggy was a toddler and he stood her up on the bar of the Squatter's Arms to sing "K-K-K-Katie". And how when a customer complained about what she found in the bread, he said "Oh, I've been looking for that cigarette butt. That'll be a halfpenny extra."

On Friday nights when the heat in the oven was just right, Uncle let people come in to bake their cakes. Sometimes they came down on Sundays and cooked their roast dinners; at Easter-time they made hot cross buns. And there were turkeys at Christmas, which was when Uncle did the hams for the Gaol. There were usually a dozen, and he'd wrap them in a jacket of bran dough, and then in brown paper, and cook them in a tray in the oven.

Five

Beauville meant street people — men in two-wheeler carts drawn by ancient horses, though the Fish Man always walked. He was an Italian with a black moustache who carried his tin tray on his shoulder. After the housewives had made their choice he'd clean the fish at their back doors.

The Terai Tea Man was English — a real Pom in his collar and tie and felt hat. Terai was flasher than Amgoorie or Paou Chung. Customers felt proud when he stopped outside their houses.

The Rabbit Man sat on a plank and called "Rabby, Rabby-oh." He had them hanging, all furry, paws tied together in pairs, over a rail at the back of his cart. The women would go out in their pinnies with their plates, and he'd rip off the skin and chop off the feet and ask if they wanted the giblets for the cat.

The butcher's cart meant a red-haired boy in a striped apron, with his money bag over his shoulder, jumping down to sharpen his knife. He was a little bit simple and wore the Beauville Football Club colours in his lapel and: "Beauvs are gunna win today," he'd always say for a greeting — it didn't matter that it wasn't Saturday, or that the footy season hadn't begun.

The greengrocer was everyone's friend. The women would stroll out and yarn as they tested the fatness of the peas, and held their babies up to stroke the horse's nose.

And twice a day, morning and afternoon, the milk-man's pannikin rattled as he measured milk into billy-cans and jugs. And there were the sing-song voices of Chinese hawkers selling teatowels and tablecloths, cucumbers and watermelons. The children whispered that if you threw a hat on the ground and spat on it a Chinaman would go mad, but when they did it nothing happened.

Charlie Dazzle came and collected people's dead animals. He used to cut them up and carry them away. No one knew where the animals were taken.

Twisty was the Ice-cream Man. He was a nice old fellow, very clean, with a white moustache. He wore a white washing hat and a white coat, and his hooded cart was drawn by a black pony. When they heard his bell, the children would run out with their pennies.

A little man, bent as a hobgoblin, brought bags of shell-grit for the garden. And there was the Dust-oh, the Bottle-oh, the Rag-and-Bone Man.

Sticky Thomas had a lolly shop on the Port Road. His other nickname was Taffy. He was a fat man with a smiling pink face. The children would walk to his shop just to look in the window. There were toffees, cinna-mon sticks, humbugs, and a special milk rock that he named Beauville Rock. Sticky loved children. He was patient as they stood before his counter with their pennies, trying to choose. Sometimes he'd let Clare have a paper cornet of common lollies for nothing. She used to watch him make toffee in his little back room. He'd mix it up in a basin, and then throw it over a hook and tug and stretch until it was like a snake in his hands. It was gold to start with, and he kept working it until it went white.

Mr Hall, the butcher, had a toupee that jumped every time he used the chopper, but he was a Michelangelo in meat. His winter window displays were famous. He could fashion a shoulder of mutton into a thing of beauty by decorating it with delicate twists and twirls of variously coloured melted fats. From a block of suet he could produce carvings of motor cars and steamers. Once he did a sailing ship floating on a churning sea of lard. His most elaborate creation was a model of the Queen of Angels' Church, cleverly reproduced in dripping.

Doodys had a shop that sold newspapers and stationery and at the back was a barber's with a layback chair, hot towels, and a cut-throat razor. Mr Doody was the Beauville SP bookie and collected the betting slips from the Gasworks Hotel. They were kept in a cigar box on the shelf in the chimney. But once the police came in by surprise and Mr Doody had to stuff the slips in his mouth.

There was a tribe of Doody children, and always a new baby in a cot. Clare thought it must be cosy sleeping three in a double bed, sometimes four, and going barefoot in summer and wearing sandshoes in winter and having baths in the copper.

Mr Doody was a heavy drinker and Mrs Doody was always giving hidings but they were a close sort of family that looked after each other and every dog they had was called Champ. There was a boys' room and a girls' room, and even going to the lavatory at night was an adventure — all giggling together down the path with the lantern. They sat on long forms to eat their dinner because there weren't enough chairs, and there were always jellies on Sundays and Albert cake with pink icing, and at Aunt Rosa's the bread and butter was thin but at Doodys' the slices were thick. When it was a heat-wave they slept on the beach, and they played draughts and ludo and cards and Mr Doody kept score on a slate that he cleaned with spit. Doodys had a cockatoo that died and they gave it a funeral. They had a wind-up gramophone with one record called "Under the Double Eagle".

Mrs Doody was famous for her plum jam, but she wasn't a loving mother. People reckoned it was because she'd been a convent girl till she was eighteen and then Mr Doody got her into trouble and her family wouldn't have anything to do with her, and when Granma Doody came to stay she walked round at night with a candle and bent over Mrs Doody in bed and said "I'll beat you yet." People said she could be a hard woman. Once when a couple of the boys got badly sunburned she hit them on the blisters, and Mr Doody used to hit her, too, and she'd scream she'd gone blind. But she could be a lady drinking shandy, and she loved going to the races, and she took all her children away from the Queen of Angels' when the priest complained about Leo Doody dropping his marbles in Mass.

Leo had to sit in the front row at school so the teacher could throw something at him or give him a clout across the ear. He used to play the wag a lot. He was the leader of a gang of little boys who were always at the river catching yabbies. Once they caught a big goldfish by the weir and an ugly spidery thing that turned into a dragonfly. They hunted lost balls on the golf-links and sold them back to the golfers, and belted rocks on the roof of the mad lady's house, and pinched fruit from the greengrocer's cart. Their favourite games were Nick-nock — that was knocking on people's doors in the dark and running — and Black Rabbit, that meant a string was tied to a door-knocker and then the boys hid and pulled the string and waited for someone to answer the door.

All the Doody boys were ginger-haired and freckled like their mother. The girls were dark and Irish looking like their father.

Beryl Doody was Clare's friend. They were in the same class at school and Beryl made the other girls stop teasing Clare because of her clothes. Clare was the only child who wore an overcoat at the Beauville school, and they laughed at her pearl buttons and socks to the knee. Before she knew Beryl, Clare was frightened to go to the lavatory. None of the school lavatories had doors, they were just open cubicles, and what if someone saw that her bloomers were embroidered and had frills?

Clare liked school after she knew Beryl. She had her little case and her books and everything, and the lessons were easy, the teacher was nice, and in winter the school shop sold saucers of hot peas with vinegar. Clare and Beryl shared bites of their apples and sat under the pepper trees in the yard and pulled the fluff off each other's jumper and rolled it in a ball and whoever had the biggest was the winner.

Beryl was a gentle girl, neat and tidy, but Aunt Rosa wouldn't allow Clare to bring her home. No one in Beauville was good enough for Auntie, now that the sign above the shop window had been changed from PRIDDLE'S BAKERY to PRIDDLE & SON — BAKERS AND CONFECTIONERS.

The SON and the CONFECTIONERS gleamed out bolder, more golden, than the other words. Ralph was kept so busy at his decorating that he didn't deliver any more. For suddenly Priddles' cakes graced tea-tables of distinction. There were Madeira cakes disguised as crinolined ladies, walnut and strawberry layer cakes, Imperial and Parisienne gâteaux. For Easter, Ralph had decided on simnel cakes ornamented with woolly chicks emerging from gilded egg shells; for Christmas there'd be fruit cakes bearing rock sugar Polar bears and holly sprays.

Even in church Aunt Rosa kept her distance from others. She came in late with an important sway, her voice hung on the hymn's final note after everyone else's had come off. Her veil fitted over her face like a mask and had a hole where her mouth was because she sucked peppermints, and often mixed them up with the coins for collection.

She called herself a lady who was meant for a sheltered life. She wouldn't have anything to do with Aunt Crystal because Uncle Jack Belcher was head barman at a city hotel.

Six

The Gasworks Hotel had windows as good as the ones in the Queen of Angels' Church. They were all little leaded panes inset with coloured glass tulip buds and roses and lilies, to make a wreath about the scarlet word BAR. When the lights came on in the pub on wintry afternoons, the clear glass turned pinkish. And BAR was printed redly, again, on the green double doors, and soon Jack Belcher's name would be over them, announcing that he was licensed to sell ales, wines and spirits.

When Aunt Crystal turned up to tell them, Aunt Rosa didn't look pleased. She said Papa would have died if he'd known — one of his daughter reduced to serving in a public bar. But he'd been dead for years, already, and Aunt Crystal seemed to regard it as a certain step up. In any case, she said, Valentine insisted. He reckoned her influence would keep the clientele orderly. Every time she mentioned Mr Arden her voice went more English. She said it was a miracle how he'd found them, just when he'd bought the hotel — just when Jack was ready for a change from the Land of Promise. Of course it meant Beauville. But the Gasworks Hotel wasn't anywhere near the gasometer, and she didn't know how Rosa could bear the pughole being so close.

Her face was white with rice powder; she had frizzy ginger hair. She was rattly with bangles and necklaces. She'd swooped on Clare with foolish cries. But her smile

158

was scary-sweet. "Just the image of Dove," she cried, but hatred peered out of her eyes. And she smelled odd. Mixed with the violetty scent smell was something oily as cough mixture, musky as incense. It was queer to be kissed by a stranger's purple mouth and patted by her lace mittens and given sixpence from her silver chain purse.

And another thing Mr Arden insisted upon, was that the Priddles and Clare should come to lunch at the hotel on the Sunday that the Belchers moved in.

The people who were moving out were Assyrians. Aunt Crystal called them the natives, but they didn't wear turbans, their skin wasn't as tanned as Uncle Jack's. The hotel broker was there, too, to conduct the little ceremony of handing over the key. Hands were shaken and there were drinks all round. Then the Assyrians departed, leaving behind them the traditional luncheon spread on the dining-room table.

There were devilled turkey legs and rhum babas, and Uncle Jack was a small man like an Italian. Every time he said "bonzer" or "beaut" Aunt Crystal winced. There were things in green jelly and Alice was a large girl with blotting-paper skin. She kept crossing and uncrossing her legs, her stockings made a silky sound, her name wasn't Belcher but Gerard. Her papa had been a member of the English aristocracy who'd gambled away a great fortune. She said it as if she knew it by heart, and every time she said a word it sounded tight and screwed up. But that was because Alice had been born in England; because she learned elocution and went to Miss Stack's private school. Alice's papa had been a soldier, but of a higher rank than Clare's. But it was a bond between them — their fathers both dying — though Alice was twelve and Clare only eight. She had

159

sausage curls and white eyelashes and there was a Princess Alice in England. Things were either swimming in sauces or dry so they wouldn't go down. Aunt Rosa said No thank you, coldly, but corks kept popping and Peggy sat all hunched in her fight against temptation but Uncle Will, Uncle Jack and Ralph drank and drank.

Aunt Rosa didn't approve of hotels, but she was glad to have Clare out of the house. So when it wasn't Doodys' it was the Gasworks Hotel, where Aunt Crystal was mistress in dignified black. She took great pride in how she presented the bar. And there were jardinières of blue gum on the landings, vases of Iceland poppies in the Ladies' Parlour and wax doilies, canine statues: the black and white Scotch terriers, the bulldog for Bulldog stout. Upstairs was a glass skylight edged with wooden rails that overlooked the parlour where ladies and gentlemen mixed. On Saturday afternoons Clare and Alice looked down. There was a wine called fourpenny dark, something called Black Velvet, and Uncle Jack was thought a good fellow in Beauville because as well as handing round Monopole cigars he was always willing to whip an egg up with Worcestershire sauce and offer it to take away the day after's sick feeling.

But sometimes a drinker would look upwards, and then Pompy would be sent to reprimand them. He was a sickly looking person with a cyst on his head; his surname was Simms; he was boots-barman. It meant he served in the bar, polished the lino in the parlours, cleaned out the yard and cellar, hosed the footpath every Monday, painted the stairs on each side of the carpet with black Easywork once a fortnight, and helped when the brewery horses came with the beer. They had brass medallions and feathery fetlocks and they'd drink from the water trough and then stand still while the brewery men in their leather aprons rolled the barrels down a ladder.

Aunt Crystal was so ladylike that she didn't believe in church because the people who attended would be common. Sunday was when Uncle Jack bottled the wine in the cellar; other days he put on his alpaca bar coat and disappeared into the place that meant men: men swearing, being sick, sometimes peeing on the floor. Aunt Crystal couldn't abide the six o'clock swill. She staved it off with gum tips and poppies, pictures of scenes: a coachman scene, a snow scene, horses and hounds. But behind everything was BAR in bright red. Big men, little men, and a six o'clock roar of voices; upside-down glasses on Turkish towelling, drip-trays under the beer-taps. Aunt Crystal took a glass of stout every morning at eleven — to buck her up, keep her going.

Uncle Jack was kind. In summer he brought Alice strawberries and ice-cream in a glass beer mug; on hot nights when she couldn't sleep he'd bring her a bottle of lemonade from the bar. But Alice was a Gerard ... Jack Belcher's family had been poor — his granny had lived in a room hollowed out of the ground, thatched with leaves and branches; she'd watched the Aborigines building their wurlies ... Robbie Gerard meant England — the deer park, the shrubbery, and Alice must never forget it. But one day she said to Clare that she had to tell someone, and now Alice's memories of England were different.

... Hettie was always sucking soda mints for her indigestion. She was Mama's girl friend, and they all lived together — Mama, Hettie, Alice — in the flat. There were yellow silk lampshades, a fleecy hearthrug, cretonne cushions to the armchairs, a picture of Flora Macdonald helping Prince Charlie to escape. Hettie said they must be respectable, but she kept having disguises. When she wore the lace bandeaux pulled down bandage-wise to just above her eyebrows, she was Madame Olga who'd been the palmist at the Piccadilly Hotel, but now she consulted at home and read girls' fortune cards and told them they were in trouble and took them under her wing. Then she was a nurse in a starched apron and she gave the girls medicine and dipped men's fingers in a bowl of soapy water and jabbed at their cuticles till the half-moons rose up on their nails. When a gentleman visited, Mama helped, too. The room was dizzy with excitement and then Mama and the man went upstairs. Laughter floated down, but there could be the same sad sound as the girls made when Hettie gave her treatments. Sometimes the man was a soldier and there might be something for Hettie's collection of war relics. She had bullets, pieces of shrapnel, a strip of canvas from Baron von Richthofen's scarlet aeroplane, a German officer's belt with *Gott mit uns* on its clasp. Hettie was patriotic and went off each week for her day at the hospital as a Red Cross worker. And one day Mama went with her and met Sergeant Belcher. He said he'd love some grapes. He didn't realize the cost of them — they were fifteen shillings a pound. It was Hettie who lent Mama the money to buy them, but she didn't come to the wedding at St George's, Hanover Square.

Seven

And Beauville was rainbow balls, liquorice babies, nullah-nullahs, fizzoes. They were all lollies you could buy at the Town Hall pictures where a lady-pianist played love and cowboy-chasing music and other ladies in skirts to the ankles sat with their hats on their laps. The larrikins in the back row threw grapes; Diver Dunn, the chucker-out, ran round with his torch. At interval the queue for the lavatory was so long that the bad boys used to cross the road and wee through the flap in the prim and proper dressmaker's front door that had the big biscuit tin for letters tacked up behind it.

Evangelists came for tent missions, the bark mill burned down, but the best fire was the one at the Eskimo Pie factory. People raced in with saucepans and filled them with ice-cream.

Summer meant the constant crack of lavatory creeper seeds bursting, like little black bullets, from their pods. Families sat on their verandahs in the dark and called good-night to passers-by.

In winter the streets were flooded. The pughole resembled a lake; boats were rowed along the Port Road, there was even a man in a bath. The children gathered at the Beauville bridge and leaned over and tried to catch the oranges that had come down from the Hills. There were cows and pigs and horses floating past, too, and a girl fell in and was drowned, and there were bunches of violets at her funeral.

One year a Maori princess came to church and Clare got her autograph; some Saturdays the footpaths were crowded with people off to the football, and if the blue and golds were losing they'd light up at the brick kiln and the smoke drifted over the oval in the hope that the visiting team wouldn't see the goal posts. Little bell flowers called one-o'clocks and two-o'clocks kept blooming in the Beauville cemetery. The Salvation Army was always on its corner by the Gasworks Hotel on Friday nights when the shops stayed open late, and Alice looked down from her window and threw pennies at her cousin, Peggy Priddle.

Sometimes the gleaming car came and surprised Clare. She'd be bundled into one of the party dresses — Arden House was the only place where she ever wore them. They hung in the wardrobe, their crinoline skirts whispering of parties with jellies and creams, an iced cake decorated with cherries, angelica, halved walnuts. The unworn dresses were taunting. Up the hill, past the golf-links, was a world of proper people; and Beryl Doody wasn't a barefoot princess, just a beggar girl whose black gipsy feet were hard as horn. Everything went flat and dull. Beauville meant the stink of gas and glue and Clare hated it. She'd been kidnapped as a baby, she didn't belong with any of the horrid people about her. The dresses made Clare feel mixed up. Mr Arden's benevolence teased and tormented her. Where did she belong? Sometimes she didn't feel that she fitted in anywhere.

Mr Tostevin was one of the oldest identities in the district. He was a patriarch with a flowing white beard and a kindly face, wrinkled and brown through long exposure to the elements. Until recently he'd been a bootblack in the city. The good old times, for him, were when there'd been ill-made roads to cover young swells' patent leather boots with mud. Mr Tostevin's hobby was building model ships. The fleet in the inland haven of his tumbledown house on the edge of the pughole comprised more than a dozen vessels, enclosed in glass cases.

A marine scene had been painted as an appropriate background to each model. Some seas were merely placidly crinkled; others flew at bows in a shower of sparks, and there were seas choked with mermaids, gangs of porpoises, spouting whales. Minutely carved figures were seen aloft or hauling on ropes. A captain peered through a telescope; a parrot perched in its cage. The beak of the bird was a small rose thorn.

Yet Mr Tostevin had never been to sea. One of the first babies born in the colony, he could remember the city when it was all tea-tree and kangaroos, terrifying black men and a scarcity of water.

He took a great liking to Alice when Clare took her to visit him. Because she'd made the journey out from England, he considered her an authority on seas and sailing ships. He did the recalling for her. Did she remember the fruits of the tropics at Rio — the custard apples and green bananas that were so refreshing after months of salt beef and bully soup? He didn't take any account of the intervening years that distanced his imaginary voyages from her real one. Alice had crossed the Line and above her head the Northern constellations had disappeared and the Southern taken their place — therefore she *must* remember: white islands rising from coral seas, the sails thrashing and bellying as they battled through the roaring forties ... his reminiscing voice didn't require an answer.

In the spring it was Mr Tostevin's ninetieth birthday, and he decided to celebrate it by taking the children to the new amusement park at the beach. Alice prepared for disappointment. It didn't seem possible that Mama would allow her the treat.

But Mr Tostevin started Crystal off on rememberings of her own. Granpa Sparks might have been just like him ... Crystal was a child again, and Daisy Sparks gathered her close and told of the pioneer who'd planted the grape-vine and ridden the white Arab horse. Crystal did the unexpected, and agreed to Alice accompanying Clare and Mr Tostevin on Saturday's outing.

And several young Doodys came, too. The sun shone and Mr Tostevin led them down the Port Road in his black Sunday suit. He kept raising his hat, for they passed so many of his cronies and acquaintances.

Soon they walked through soursobby paddocks. Tadpoles flickered in a creek and Leo Doody stopped to hunt liquorice root. Almond blossom drifted on to soft green barley grass. Beryl Doody turned cartwheels; Annie Doody chased Alice.

They came to the Chinese market-gardens and, behind the windbreak fringe of bamboos, were sure they saw stooping pigtailed figures who waited to give them the evil eye. Then they wrinkled their noses and walked faster, for the fertile soil was top-dressed with rabbit heads and guts.

Arden House rose up in the distance. Once, said Mr Tostevin, the place didn't have that name. An old sea captain had lived there and the birds had been safe. But when the captain died and Valentine Arden purchased the estate, everything changed. He must own the birds' silky bodies and bright feathers, their fluted song and wheeling flight. He collected the wagtail's mincing scuttle, the magpie's chatterbox voice; the speckled feather, the eager eye, the small chirrup of content. And Valentine Arden let the men with their guns come and warm bodies, quick with life, fell from the sky. Every month on the estate there was a pigeon shoot.

At last they came to the beach. The sea was as placid as glass. Mr Tostevin gazed wistfully at a line of limp-sailed yachts and suggested a stroll to the end of the jetty, but they pulled him on towards the amusement park.

"This way, this way," called a papier-mâché head, and they saw sparkling domes and tapering minarets, and the high sweeping lines of the Big Dipper. The roundabout horses circled to wheezy organ tunes, and Adiva — loveliest woman in the world and Australia's Wild Water Lily — swam in the aquarium with the Giant Golden Schnapper. There was a mystic from the Orient, suspiciously twangy of tongue and white of neck beneath his Eastern swarthiness, and it said THE GIRL IN THE BLOCK OF ICE but she only lay on top shivering in her bathers, and Mr Tostevin hurried them past Vanessa the Undresser.

And then they were waylaid by a little old man. His eyes were filmed with age, his liver-spotted hands curiously knotted; one hideously deformed foot dragged behind him. He lured them into his Electric Studio with his throaty whisper for he was that prince of cajolers, the photographer. Two shilling was all he asked — "... and done while you wait, a speaking likeness." And he told Alice she'd click tonight, and said he wouldn't mind being her boy himself. But it was Leo Doody who sat beside her on the out-size cutout of the crescent moon, and tinsel stars twinkled, and Mr Tostevin watched as the other children huddled round them. Outside it was still 1928, but in the tent (as the little cripple hobbled towards the tripod and shrouded himself away beneath its cape of black cloth, and the ancient camera surveyed them) it could have been any year. They felt magically timeless, as if they'd stay children for ever. They'd always be as strong and fresh as they were now. And they held their breaths to stay perfectly still, and smiled into the camera's cold eye.

Eight

Every morning the collectors set off early with their billy carts and prams to see what they could find. There were always men down the pughole scraping round for bits of metal; and they scoured paddocks for bones, pounced on empty bottles and newspapers. They collected coal from along the railway line, driftwood off the beach, cow-pats from the parklands and manure from the lane. They snitched fruit when the greengrocer wasn't looking and pinched washing from backyard clothes-lines; they hopped the fence of the timber yard, and carted off palings and pickets, in the never-ending search for wood.

The Depression had come and everything had turned topsy-turvy. The daytime Beauville had stopped belonging to the women in their pinnies. There were unemployed men sitting at home day after day — playing cards, studying the horses for a threepenny bet. And they sat on the edge of the footpath and stood in groups outside the pubs. And other men with fibre suitcases came to the door and tried to sell needles and moth-balls, corn cures, shoe-laces, jelly powders, spices.

The newspapers told how mothers were daily besieging the charitable institutions of the city with tales of pitiful plight. They told about the women with white faces, the children gnawing crusts, the evening meals of bread and dripping, tomato sauce, golden syrup, condensed milk.

Aunt Rosa said that while people could get bread and something to scrape on it they would not starve. She said there was sadness, there was suffering, but there was vast satisfaction in bearing life.

It was a world of paupers' funerals, mutton sickness, plum jam. People queued for pink ration tickets every fortnight, and the Governor and his Lady distributed oranges, and the Beauville fashion was patches on patches and overcoats for blankets and cardboard soles to shoes. Some children dressed in wheat bags; and there was a boy who only had girl's clothes to wear, and a father and son who shared a pair of shoes. Families came home to find the furniture in the street as if by magic: the little cane chair, the chamber-pot — everything; people were always shifting, doing moonlight flits, because they couldn't pay the rent. There were epidemics of measles, whooping cough, bronchitis, boils, chilblains, running noses, cold sores, head lice, ringworm, sore eyes. The electricity kept being cut off so it was back to kerosene lamps and candles; or people sat in the dark or went to bed at sunset. In the winter of 1931, men made a ragged army as they roamed the city in tunics and greatcoats left over from the war. The coats had been dyed blue — but badly, so they were a queer shade of red.

But some lived on velvet. Up the hill, past the golf-links, there were doctors and dentists and lawyers and ladies who arranged bowls of Golden Emblem roses. Up there the fashions were different to Beauville's. White fox fur gave a snowball effect; chromium was the rage for jewels.

It was as if there were two cities. In the first there was order, well-being and industry; in the second, starvation, unemployment and misery.

The newspapers ran contests and competitions. The contest for the best knitteds to clothe the babies of the poor. The competition for the most economical and nourishing three-course dinner to help poor householders. The Christmas cake and plum pudding competition that would provide something in the nature of a feast for poor families. Readers were urged to subscribe to the Blanket Appeal and the Needy Children's Hot Dinner Fund.

Every time there was a write-up about the poverty in Beauville, the cars would come down the hill. A link was provided between rich and poor, and some of the latter said it was glorious and there were squeals of delight at the cars driven by chauffeurs in livery. But it was the gentleman and lady in the back seat who stepped out and came into the little houses for a look at the shocking conditions. They were so nice as they inspected the empty larders and the wheat bags for bedclothes, the newspapers between blankets for warmth. For a few days the houses they visited were full of food. Some of the poor said it was wonderful that the rich people should come down and treat them as if they were friends and not remind them that, after all, they might be in want through their own fault. But others had envious eyes and no sense of their place and no manners. It was disgraceful how they weren't grateful when one of the motor fleet of mercy stopped at their door.

Valentine Arden was often to be seen in Beauville, now. He was a familiar figure, day and night. He braved even the narrowest ill-lit streets, where the little houses were the dirtiest and smelled to make you sick. He didn't seem to mind the swarms of ragged children or the roaring raving drunks or the knock shop. He walked by the gasometer, the pughole, and past all the pubs on the

Port Road, all the shops. He inspected the plate of cream lilies that looked more like sponge snails in the window of Priddles' Bakery; he walked past the pickle factory, the brewery, and gazed at the oily surface of the river. Even the children's crooked hopscotch squares, chalked like secret messages on the footpath, didn't escape his notice.

None of the locals went to Priddles' for their bread any more. They took their ration tickets to the baker on the Port Road. They felt he was one of them. He gave them free hot cross buns at Easter and displayed a special cake in his window every Friday during the football season. The cake's blue and gold icing predicted the scores of Saturday's game between Beauvs and their opponents. If its predictions had come true, Beauville would have won every time.

Priddle & Son was high class, and catered for the élite up the hill. Will Priddle wasn't allowed in the bake-house, now, because he couldn't be trusted — the rich people had started complaining about string in their bread, and Ralph said he did it on purpose, and so Will spent each day at the Gasworks Hotel.

Peggy had been banished, too, because she'd mis-behaved herself with Pompy Simms. The boots-barman had seen her at one of the Salvation Army sing-songs and next thing he was going off to Knee Drill and Holi-ness Meeting. Peggy had saved a soul, even though Pompy still served behind the bar. She wore his ring from Woolworth's round her neck on a ribbon next to the camphor bag and the rabbit-skin bib. And Pompy knelt at the penitence form and testified under the JESUS

SAVES motto on the wall. Peggy still went to bed clutching the shawl that was bait for God's baby. But when it came there was no rejoicing. It all happened different to Peggy's dreams. She'd been Uncle's little thoroughbred, but she got put out in the street like a pet they didn't want.

And the Depression meant *The Princess and the Plumber*, and Greta Garbo in *Romance* and Norma Shearer in *Let us be Gay*. For the talkies had come and the Wondergraph's commissionaire wore scarlet and gold, the Regent's, royal blue. There were usherettes in apple-blossom pink and the night crowds came in evening dress, and boiled shirts glistened, but more and more musicians went on the breadline as the theatre orchestras were disbanded.

For a while the streets were thronged with wandering minstrels: harpists, violinists and flautists; banjoists, mouth organists and steel guitarists. There were brass and string bands, and a blind man played the concertina by the Bank of New South Wales and Piccolo Pete was outside the post office. Men played Jew's harps and juggled oranges, but somehow it was too sad — it made the shoppers feel guilty and profits went down — so the City Council decided the buskers should be banned.

Nine

Leo Doody was one of the Beauville Boys. These boys just did things together. They played cards in the shed, and two-up and billiards; they fought each other, sold papers for Leo's dad, and knocked the cones from the pine trees in the parklands to get the monkey nuts.

Leo went through to Grade Seven at the Beauville school. The school band dressed in white, with a little white hat turned up at the side, and Leo always wanted to join it. And he had a flute given to him and he was determined to be in the band, and then somehow he was, and he was putting his fingers up and down on the flute pretending to play. But he couldn't, so they chucked him out.

And the Beauville Boys had swimming holes along the river: the Rocky, the Leechy, the Loggy. The Loggy was the best, and they used to bank the river up with rocks. You could see the Rocky from the Beauville bridge. The leeches were like slugs, and they caught yabbies, too, in a net with a piece of meat on a string. They'd cook them and eat them, though they weren't very nice — not as good as crab. And they caught tadpoles and blew up frogs — put a straw in the frog's tail and blew. There were two-up schools by the red railway bridge. The Beauville Boys were given a shilling to be cockatoos and watch for a raid, and when the police came the men would run into the river.

When Leo went to the Beauville Mission camp at the

beach he took his clothes with him in a sugar bag that his mum had made into a haversack with straps. He had to drop out of the school football team because he didn't have boots. It was his ambition to have a push-bike.

And the Beauville Boys pulled a bloke out of the river by the weir — he'd eaten a lot of apricots before he started swimming and must have got cramps. And they milked the cows in the saleyards at the back of the Gaol, and knocked the electric lights out with their shanghais. They chased the horses in the parklands and cut their tails off and sold them to the saddlers and the brush people; they went shoplifting at Woolworth's, and pinched watermelons from the Chinese gardens — stuck them up their jumpers and ran. The Chinese used to chase them and fire saltpetre from a shot-gun.

Leo played the wag from school a lot, and then he was fourteen and could leave. He'd sold newspapers round Beauville from the time he was ten; when he sold them at the brewery they'd give him a little glass of beer. Now he branched out big time and sold in the city. The fellow who managed the newspaper boys was a fight promoter. He promoted the Alabama Kid. And he was a lover-boy, with a girl friend as well as a wife, and he owned a racehorse called Silver Dash.

Sometimes Clare walked with Leo along the path above the river. Below them, the unemployed men's huts on the river-bank made a village that stretched from the weir to the back of the zoo — a distance of a mile and a half. The huts were made of scraps of tin and hessian bags. Some were just shanties with the bags rotting from constant exposure to all weathers, but others were presentable little homes with the hessian whitewashed to look like canvas, and there was even one painted red with white lines to represent bricks. And some had fireplaces built of bricks collected from rubbish dumps, chipped to correct size, and then bound together with pug from the river. About the huts patches of ground had been cleared, in which thrived tomatoes and melons, lettuces, onions, potatoes, and even strawberries. It was not only to vegetables that the men had turned their attention. Here and there hollyhocks, sunflowers and geraniums flourished behind fences of split bamboos.

One of the unemployed men was Old Bill, who'd fought in the Boer War, and again in the Great War with the Lancashire Fusiliers. Once Clare and Leo had stopped to talk to him as, soapsuds to the elbow, he washed his socks in a petrol tin. Front-line trenches, he said, were preferable to idleness on the banks of a river. "One has to beg for one's life here," he said. "Over there it was a gamble with death. I won, but now what of the future?"

Another of the men by the river was Poker Roberts, who played poker with his dog almost every afternoon and usually won hundreds of pounds from him at a sitting. And Eggy Mitchell had a weakness for eggs, and constantly robbed all the birds' nests he came across and devoured the contents. And Gentleman Jones was popularly supposed to be a product of Oxford — he had the real Oxford bleat and could quote the classics like a professor. He wore a straw boater, and a collar and tie. The collars, of which he seemed to have an inexhaustible supply, were paper ones. When they became black with dirt he threw them away. The rest of his attire was mostly rags.

The Joker made a living cutting empty kerosene tins into ornamental pot-stands. They were dainty and lacy and he sold them for two shillings each. He lived in the gabled canvas hut that was camouflaged to resemble red brick. An odd sort of fellow, he was friends with Leo, but hardly spared Clare a glance. When his mouth wasn't screwed up in its twisted smile, the Joker looked something like a gawky overgrown boy himself.

A block of wood did for his cutting table. His hands looked clumsy, but under them the tin became a fantastic thing, flounced and ruffled and pleated, fretted with roses and true-lovers' knots.

Then Leo started coughing. He didn't cough much, but Mrs Doody didn't like it, and he ate a terrible lot but he didn't get any fatter. But Leo said he was all right and went on selling his newspapers. Then one night he got caught in the rain, and his cough grew worse. But his complexion was beautiful, transparent looking, with bright red cheeks — but he was very moody. Then one night he was so bad that Mrs Doody thought it was pneumonia. When the doctor came he said: "His ankles are very swollen and once the ankles start to swell there's not much hope."

Mrs Doody tried to fatten Leo up with milk emulsion and rice pudding. She kissed her rosary beads and slept with them under her pillow. But nothing did any good. Leo was bringing up horrible white stuff, and Mrs Doody used to have to keep everything that he used — all the plates and everything — separate. She used to take the white phlegmy stuff and throw it in a hole in the yard and put lime on it and burn it. When they got the results of the X-ray they said it was consumption, a galloping sort that didn't take long. It was in both lungs and they couldn't do anything. They said it was the worst case they'd seen and Leo went into hospital.

Mrs Doody took him in dishes of his favourite steak and kidney pie, even on a Sunday when the buses didn't run and she had to walk all the way in to the city and back. For a while he didn't seem too bad. Then one Saturday the police came to the shop and said Mrs Doody was wanted at the hospital immediately. When she got there, Leo was in a coma and they didn't think he'd come out of it and they were waiting for the doctor. Mrs Doody waited and waited and she was sitting there and suddenly Leo came to. He said "Where's the *News*?" Mrs Doody said "What do you want the *News* for?" He said "I want to put something on a horse, I want to have a look at the races." It didn't seem to be Leo speaking, it seemed like his father, but to keep him quiet Mrs Doody had to go and get a *News*. When the doctor came he was sitting up in bed reading it, picking out the winners for the next race.

Anyway, he died on a Wednesday. They sent for Mr and Mrs Doody, but Leo was dead when they got there. He'd gone thin, and to Mrs Doody when he was dead he looked like a parrot and she couldn't bear to look at a parrot for years afterwards.

Ten

Doodys' house had been more home to Clare than the one beside the bakery. She'd loved the evenings when they sat round the big table with its ruby velvet cloth and did jigsaws and played cards. The youngest Doodys would be curled up on the rug like sleepy puppies, and Mr Doody would sit in his chair and rustle the newspaper and smoke his pipe. There'd be the click of knitting needles, the lazy flicker of the fire and the small explosions of sparks; there always seemed to be a vase of overblown daisies dropping their pollen.

But now Leo was dead. Since he'd died, his mother's ginger hair had gone white. And then the police came in their Flying Squad motor cars to raid the barber's shop, and Beryl started work at the egg factory where she inspected eggs under a powerful electric light for green yolks, blood spots and worms.

But Clare went to the high school in the city. She wore a navy-blue uniform, and there were stripes on her hatband and an emblem on her pocket. She kept her stockings up with garters and was learning Latin and French while Beryl sorted bad eggs from good ones. Aunt Rosa said that if it hadn't been for Mr Arden they'd never have been able to afford it. When Peggy misbehaved herself and became the unmentionable who married Pompy Simms, someone had to take her place serving in the bakery. Thanks to Mr Arden it wasn't Clare, but Betsy Dew from next door.

Those evenings at Doody's seemed like a dream ... the playing-card castles rose up from the velvet tablecloth, the jigsaw pieces fretted together, in the corner was the specimen case Mr Doody had made to display his pieces of gold and copper, silver and crystal collected when he was a miner at Broken Hill. He'd carved all the fancy bits with a penknife, he'd worn the skin off the top of his fingers sandpapering them, and only he knew the secret of how to get the pane of glass out to open it. But when the Depression came even the treasured specimen case was sold. And Beryl seemed like a stranger.

But the suburb was still Beauville. The men came down the little streets in their carts; Sticky Thomas and the Michelangelo in Meat were open for business on the Port Road. The spire of the Queen of Angels' Church still cowed the sky with its burnished cross — the children saw it from their schoolroom windows and heard its bell toll the hours; it was as much a part of every football match at the Beauville oval as the brick-yard chimney and the weaving shadows, the umpire's whistles, the blue and gold cheers and boos, the hurtling heroes' bodies, the sheeny green grass — it was there in the distance overlooking everything; there, towering in close-up as the Catholics went inside to make holy water signals and jabber in a foreign tongue.

Clare walked out each day in her high school uniform and Beauville shrank from her. Once each patch of front garden, each slippery slab of verandah had been an old friend — and this was the house with the fernery; that, the one with the twin pomegranate trees and the children used to pinch the pomegranates coming home from school. And each front window was a neighbourly stage with its looped lacy curtains, its hovering I-spy face, its sleepy curled-up cat or vase of flowers. But not now.

Now Clare had lost the trick of seeing individual detail — all the windows looked alike, they'd all turned threatening, and the faces watched her with a frown.

On summer evenings people still came out of their houses to talk. The women would sit on the doorsteps, the men would squat in the gutter with glasses of beer. Gangs of children whooped round the streets, playing hide-and-seek and chasey. They were the children who were given free books and free shoes and a ticket for free dinners at the Mission. Clare wished she were one of them. She envied them going to the Mission where the soup was made in a copper; she even liked the girls' ugly black strap shoes that fastened with buttons.

The only friend Clare had in Beauville, now, was Alice. They spent a lot of time in her room at the Gasworks Hotel. There were muslin ruffles and bunches of cherries on the wallpaper, but it was the wrong sort of room for Alice. She had a woman's body but Aunt Crystal dressed her like an out-of-date child, and the sausage curls made her heavy face resemble that of an old king of France. She wanted to listen to Uncle Jack's stories; she wanted to say "bonzer" and "beaut". She lived in a pub but she mustn't set foot in the bar. It was because of having had an aristocratic father — even Alice's sanitary towels were of such fine linen that they might have done for serviettes. Alice just wanted to be ordinary, the same as other Beauville people. She was tired of remembering that she was Robbie Gerard's daughter. She wanted to cut her hair, get a job, go dancing at the Blue Danube Ballroom where the latest stunt between foxtrots was a pie-eating contest.

Sometimes Clare and Alice talked about their fathers. Robbie Gerard and Travice Thorn had both made the supreme sacrifice; they lay somewhere in France and one was an Australian hero, the other was English ... not flesh on barbed wire but lines of snowy crosses, Remembrance Day poppies, names carved in lasting bronze.

Clare and Alice had stood together, part of a hushed multitude on Anzac Day, to witness the unveiling of the State War Memorial ... The Diggers strode proudly along to quickstep tunes and the tinkle-tinkle of medals. And there was the skirling of bagpipes and the army nurses in their scarlet capes, but it was ruined by the motor cars laden with blind and maimed soldiers — War stopped being a gala day, and the Diggers in their civvies were beginning to show their years. Time had touched with grey many of their heads and some civilian suits were shabby because the wearers had been workless for months.

But then it was impressive again with the chaplains offering prayers, and orations amplified by loud speakers. When the Governor pulled the cord that dropped the flags from the front of the monument there was thunderous applause as the bronze figures representing Youth were seen gazing up at the great marble-winged angel, symbolic of Sacrifice. After the "Last Post" and the "Reveille", the Governor laid a laurel wreath and then private persons filed up to add their offerings. Clare gazed at the sea of faces stretching into the distance — faces of mothers whose sons slept at Gallipoli, in France, or other war zones; faces of Diggers whose mates would never more clasp their hands; faces of thousands whose loved ones' names were recorded in the shrine of the memorial.

And Clare and Alice would talk of their mothers.

... Dove was a lady like a ghost who walked in the garden at Arden House. She was a pale moth in her smoke-grey dress, and her white hands hovered above the flowers. Clare hated the little smile on her mouth, her small careful steps, her gentle voice. Dove liked painting wild flowers. Her slender white hands captured the fluffy lightness of the wattle, the feathery delicacy of gum blossom. Her brush made a *ping* as she swilled it in water that turned cloudy as her hands welcomed Clare. Then they'd walk in the garden and eat sugared cakes in the drawing-room and Mr Arden would watch them, smiling. Dove seemed so far away; she was the ghost, the moth, a princess in a tower.

It didn't seem possible that Dove Thorn and Crystal Belcher were sisters.

... Crystal was in the sitting-room at the Gasworks Hotel with Mr Arden. Alice listened at the door. "Hettie wrote again," she heard him say. Crystal didn't answer, but she was queer all afternoon. Johnnie Walker was a perfect gentleman, the whisky sparkled golden in the glass, but the smell on her breath was awful. Then she was in the bedroom and Jack Belcher was pounding on the door. She was a sick person, coughing up, and she said words she should never have known and then Jack Belcher was slapping her quiet. Faded memories teased at Alice's mind. Snow whirled like confetti, past the window was a world of swansdown, and there was a man with a black moustache, a man all ginger like a cat ... tinker, tailor, soldier ... When Mama and the man went upstairs, Hettie would play with Alice — they played Spillikins and told riddles and Hettie sang "Be my little baby bumble-bee". And she told fortunes and sucked soda mints. But who was she?

Eleven

Across the greens the winter sunlight shifted and died. A blob of orange moving slowly on a distant slope resolved itself into a brilliant beret. A white ball skipped into sight. Milady was on the golf-links.

Spring brides entered churches in satin with long sleeves. Flowers, pets and babies went on show. All-red ensembles were in evidence at race meetings.

On a summer's night, shadowy boats glided to and fro with their cargo of pleasure seekers. "There she goes," someone shouted and the river carnival's first rocket tore a fiery streak in the sky, paling the moon in its brightness. There were fireworks like curtain cascades, rainbows, tropical flying fish, twinkling stars. It was a brilliant two pound a minute display, and the night went on and on.

Then, despite deepest depression, it was Happy New Year, 1932. That midnight the city's young male element formed a serpentine march outside the Town Hall; couples danced everywhere with funny little hats on their heads. Beauville stayed the same with its slums and pugholes. As hungry men queued outside the Salvation Army free meal kitchen, and the zoo lions roared as more shanties went up along the river, Valentine Arden decided to give a party.

And so a special three-tiered cake was ordered from Priddles'. Ralph felt the elaborately piped edifice would be his masterpiece. When baking was done, he sprinkled on orange-flower water, rum and brandy, then brushed each top with heated apricot jam. Then almond paste was applied, then two coats of royal icing of a perfect and dazzling whiteness that Ralph rubbed with fine sandpaper to get quite smooth. Then he took up his piping bag and worked to Mr Arden's instructions. It was as if he did finest embroidery. He made zigzags and scallops and dots, feathery plumes and scrolls and a pattern of lattice. Over the latticework sprawled a grape-vine. Ralph piped with his little finger cocked and his tongue out, and followed Mr Arden's diagram dutifully. When the last grape was bunched in, the three cakes were united by Parian china pillars to make one. In the centre of the top tier Ralph placed his *pièce de résistance*: a fragile gum-paste cage that enclosed a minute sugar bird.

Rosa put their invitation to the party on the mantelpiece and started dreaming. She saw it like one of those balls she'd never gone to as a girl, with wicked champagne and ices and muslin dressing-tables in the cloakroom. And there'd be lobster salad, oyster patties, and Papa was her partner for the "Thine Alone Waltz". Rosa refused to remember how, in the old days, he'd ignored her. She wouldn't recall those queer marks on his back and the way people whispered. She made up a Papa who never touched a drop; she sponged away every stain from his black suit with weak tea; she tidied him up and made him a Methodist but even in dreams he defied her. He broke through her neat imaginings to tower over her, thrillingly uncouth, and Rosa shivered and wished Will could be like him.

She was tired of being dingy and careworn and miserable and nothing had meaning, not even the ladies and gentlemen — important people, in touch with eventful lives in need of cakes surmounted by crossed cricket bats, yale keys, silver slippers — who pressed against the counter in the shop. What had happened to Will's dreaming, why couldn't he be a man like Papa? Rosa was sick of being a veritable gunpowder magazine of a woman, all fiery sparks and quick explosions. She was constantly stamping her foot, clenching her hands, and her underwear was a dull shade of blotting-paper pink. Ralph was her darling, but there seemed no stepping stones to better things — in her eyes her boy could do no wrong, but why was he so often with Betsy Dew?

Somehow the world had crept in-between Rosa and her Saviour; it was insinuating, she couldn't keep it in its proper place. Rosa hated Betsy with her bold ways and bright eyes almost as much as she'd hated the child Dove. That mite with her hair like pale silkworms' silk had possessed power to change even the Hills. After Dove was born, home went dark and sombre; strange shadows lurked among the trees. When Rosa was married, nobody cried. She thought Will Priddle could make up for Papa's indifference, but she made a foolish choice and had eaten rue pie ever since. It had turned her over-exacting and full of whims, with an irritating inclination to nag. And what if Ralph left her? Rosa moaned into her handkerchief at the thought, and knew it could happen. Papa's chin had been jutting; Will's was retreating; Ralph's was softly fat and double, which indicated sensuousness and an indolent temperament.

Rosa worried all the time. Each day was ruined from its start. Clare Thorn was a perpetual reminder. She was the image of her mother and Rosa hated her being in the house. But Mr Arden paid to have her with them, and his money kept Priddles' afloat in perilous times, his recommendation brought them custom from up the hill. But Rosa's mouth was grudging from breakfast-time on; her terrible eye followed Clare as she dipped into the marmalade jar or helped herself to butter. She treated the child as an intruder, whose every bite and sup were a dead loss to be resented. Rosa was paid money to keep up the pretence that Travice Thorn had died in the war. Because of a lie, she felt her soul was besmirched and that doom lay all about her. She took Mr Arden's money — she did it for Ralph, but he wasn't grateful as he went across to the pub with his father and betrayed her with Betsy Dew. Envy was eating Rosa up. There was Betsy, queening it in the shop. There was Dove, living in comfort at Arden House. There was Crystal, in her cheap finery and pinchbeck jewellery, serving in a public bar — but she had Jack Belcher for a husband, a man like an Italian, with brown arms and hardly a wrinkle on his face.

Crystal didn't want to go to the party, even though if she went she'd wear black lace with rose-pink velvet puff sleeves. But of course she wouldn't attend; Valentine's teasing demanded a snub. He was all the time on about Hettie. Though how he'd unearthed her, Crystal couldn't imagine. He kept hinting that she was coming — though that was ridiculous, for Hettie was in England with all the other unmentionables from Crystal's past. It was cruel of Valentine to hint she might come. Crystal constantly felt a little *mauvaise*; she had a fearful headache and felt so tormented that she was afraid to go out of the hotel. She was sure people stared at her in the street and what would Hettie Hunt look like now? Perhaps she was that blowsy woman watching from the seat at the bus-stop, or that creature with untidy hair hovering in Sticky Thomas's doorway. The street wasn't safe and so Crystal kept inside the hotel, but it was agony serving in the bar — staying ladylike with diamanté clips while all about her were gulping throats.

Crystal couldn't stop thinking of London, of the sneering English faces that saw through her disguise, that branded her a jumped-up colonial, a slavey of an ambitious turn who'd aimed at being a lady and studied French out of a well-thumbed grammar and conjugated *avoir* and *être* in a low tone to herself as she polished the grates or blackened the shoes. After sailing all that way, a hope cherished for years had crumbled into ruins. Crystal had reached the dreamland at last, but she was still a servant — it seemed impossible to escape the dispensations of Providence. London was a cold place, its bricks and mortar snubbed her; she was lost among street cries and the rumble of cabs and omnibuses. She had the legacy from Papa's dying, but she wasn't brave enough to cut free. In London, Crystal was a lady's-maid not a lady, and she gave faithful and loyal service, and on her day off visited Cleopatra's Needle, the Albert Memorial, the Duke of Wellington's statue, the Duke of York's column. She was so close to the life she longed for, but so far away — but she was too proud to give in and sail back to the life she'd scorned. She went on writing the letters to Rosa; the dreamland was real, then, and she was lonely being in it by herself, so she made up a gentleman in her mind — a tall man with a high nose and a habit of walking about with a book in his hand. He read Tennyson to her in a deep-voiced murmur, and promised her a fine house in Belgravia with trophies of the chase on its walls, a country seat that a nobleman might be proud of, and *carte blanche* to lavish what she liked on servants, equipage and dress. A secret unrest possessed her. She lay in her lady's-maid's bed and shut her eyes and pretended that the hands trailing her body were his, not her own; she even whispered the tender love words for him; she even gave him a name: Robbie Gerard.

He seemed so real that Crystal determined to run all risks, disregard all warnings, and set her heart on finding him. She gave in her notice and dressed for conquest in silk and velvet. But he was never in the streets, nor was there much of the ideal about lodgings. Papa's money couldn't last for ever. A lean purse could not command a palace, so Crystal lived in a Maida Vale boarding-house and sat down at table with her inferiors who talked tediously about the price of butter. The women didn't count, but she mourned over the men's want of polish, the absence of the little courtesies. She was red-haired and plain; she looked forward to an old age of ever increasing gloom. Her mind rushed in a whirl as she pulled the neck of her dress lower and dabbed on rouge and then the new lodger came. He was just a lad from the country, but he had a clearly-cut profile, a fine colour; he was well-disposed, good-natured: he would do. She took the young man under her motherly wing; she was as bold as a coquette. There was scandalous tittle-tattle in the other lodgers' eyes as she petted and made much of him. He would visit her in her box of a room. She sat on the bed, he took the basket chair, and he was a sensitive, too: they'd talk of Rome and Naples, and sigh sadly as they reflected how improbable it was that they should ever see the Colosseum or bend over the blue depths of the far-famed bay. He might have been her little brother, but one evening her body was trembling out of her clothes and his face went sharp and blind, it was like dogs, and even as they did it the glamour that her passion had thrown over him passed away. He wasn't Robbie Gerard, just a boy of low birth with knowing fingers as they squirmed on the counterpane, doing the vulgar uncultured thing that was meant to be drinking the cup of pleasure to its dregs.

Then he was evasive; then he was gone. And ripe fruit did not drop into one's mouth unsought — Crystal had only herself to blame. She'd desired above all things to be like other people, but she'd reversed the order of nature in seeking him, it was for the man to seek the woman, and now she was more of an outsider than ever. As her belly grew bigger and it was harder to lace her secret away beneath her corsets, she felt smaller. She might have been a child again ... and Little Fauntleroy circled her, jeering, and then she was lost in the dark as a baby cried, and it was a monster who stole Mama away and caused her to die; and if Mrs Arden hadn't seen Dove, Crystal would have been an heiress with a sentimental love brooch at her collar and Hettie Hunt would never have entered her life ...

Dear Robbie was an aristocrat who died in the war. It didn't seem a lie, it seemed true. Hettie had hated Crystal when she left her for Jack Belcher. Jack never suspected, he was proud to have married a lady. But Hettie knew everything.

Really, Dove's mind was full of riff-raff, it was the fault

of her shut-up life. "You'd be the biggest Jonah this side of the black stump," someone said. She tried to forget, but there was a ghost inside her, remembering: summer hedges snowed over with blossom, a tree of butterflies, a gentle voice singing of silver moon, fruitful field, gates of pearl, lamb of God.

Dove watched them preparing for the party. Something had snapped inside her head and there was a panic feeling in her throat. It stopped being the drawing-room as objects disappeared. They carried the furniture away and rolled up the thick pile carpet into which feet sank noiselessly. It was all the fault of the heavily gilt and monogrammed invitation cards. The black and gold drawing-room was transformed into a veritable fairy-land by exquisite floral decorations, and scores of live birds in full song concealed among masses of flowers, vines and plants.

The voices kept sounding in her head. "All it deserved," cried one, and then: "Jesus, they got the wind, they're not using it." But then a body dodged like greased lightning, it flung itself, steadied, and then the ball made a goal, and it was the beginning of Dove's ruin. They danced the Alberts, the Lancers on a hill called Paradise, and she didn't want to remember but she couldn't stop. How bodies meant only pain for they didn't last and Daisy Sparks, Ebenezer Sparks, were just names in a cemetery and little lead letters could fall off, lichen could scab sense away. Even a child as fat as butter could die and when Bobby smiled, his fat cheeks squeezed his eyes shut but then he was still and white, a marble child on a tomb and honeysuckle was a terrible flower. An old lady sat counting the knobs in her arms, they went to her heart, and Dove couldn't stand it. She would make up for Bobby, be a child again herself —

191

but her body played cheat and sheltered another intruder and even glory vine glowing transparent in the sun couldn't keep away the danger of an older country. Behind the orchards and spotted cows, the gum trees pressed closer — once the land had been different and Dove had always sensed the danger of the soft grey flannel flower, the papery everlastings. Abandoned in the Hills, she would never feel anything again. Once long shadows had trailed his body on the oval; the windows at the back of the grandstand in the one big town he played at blazed glassily; she stared into the sun — they were like warriors dancing. But in the end he wasn't good enough, there was no one to pick up the crumbs.

Travice became George; George became Travice. United by romantic name and heroic death they made a perfect phantom husband who cancelled out two flawed fleshly men. But Dove cried each night in bed beside Clare and kept moving from town to town, in half-unconscious search of the real Travice Thorn. But it was crying for the moon. Those lonely questing years led on to more aloneness and Clare sent off to an orphanage. Dove had been destined for a heroine's life — she thought she'd found it with Mr Lovibond. She never met anyone to match his fine clerical cloth and culti-vated voice until Valentine Arden sought her out.

It was a time when Dove's courage had failed her utterly, she was not at all well; her head ached, she was listless and faded; from morning till evening she was a human machine; today was like yesterday, and to-morrow like today; for years it hadn't seemed to matter what became of her or what she did ... Valentine Arden spoke compassionately as he explained who he was. Mrs Arden had charged him with the task of finding Dove.

In offering to help her, he paid a debt to the past.

Dove had always made airy castles in her mind; she'd always planned to be a great lady. Now it seemed she had her chance. He invited her to live at Arden House, and she pictured herself as that fashionable fine lady, and also as someone happy and innocent in a world that was beautiful and sinless. Yet, as she accepted his proposal, it seemed that she turned away finally from the things of her youth, and that Travice was gone for ever.

The peacocks wailed, but she ignored them. The days went by pleasantly in the warm scented atmosphere of the house. There was a subtle charm in being watched over and petted. But he played an underhand game.

Dove was mistaken if she thought she was safe. For, at the back of everything — even Arden House — was a grim underworld that waited, like a grabbing hand, to get her. It was a desolate region where there were ragged people and stale puddles and spit in the gutter; where factory chimneys cast a pall of sickly smoke and slum houses huddled together and the soft velvet kitten mewed piteously as the yellow river swirled it on. This dark underside of living had always been there, it was a trap that had cut off countless lives. It was a terrible place, it was the world Dove read of when the newspaper stopped being respectable and told about the girl who lay strangled in long grass, a stocking fixed over her mouth. The little neat words had power — they jumped off the page, they frightened her when she lay in bed at night. Valentine's voice could do the same thing.

He knew of her lie about Travice. He could send Dove away. And where would she be then?

She was no longer mistress of herself or the situation. Luxury made the world look different — she could never go back to the old shabby life. She was a poor thing, she was lost.

But safety was hot coffee in a pretty cup, a mother o' pearl tea-caddy, a white tablecloth. He looked at her with the appraising glance of a would-be purchaser, and Dove let him make her his toy. But, really, they might have been married. Sometimes he seemed almost fond of her. But she didn't like him — she didn't like him a bit. He wronged her, he quite owned her soul. Sometimes, when he wanted to hurt her most, he talked of Arden Valley. It stopped being a green leafy place where Lady's Fingers and Black Emperors dangled. The wine bubbled and seethed in the vats; at vintage-time the grape juice dripped from laden waggons like blood. And Mrs Arden was a horror — her face merged with her neck, she was bloated, like a half-melted wax doll; and Dove wasn't a dear little baby. He said she'd been worse than a monkey, all screwed up and red.

Twelve

It was a company of knowing ones. Every man had a shrewd face. Some of them were jovial and puggy, others were hard and foxy, but all of them were knowing.

The garden had just been watered; a dizzy sound came from the ferns. They smelled the pomp of standard roses. Grass blades quivered, a flower bed was ruined as they passed over it. A stone angel surprised them; for a while they were lost. The crickets' voices swelled to warn silently. Gravel crunched, then they were back on velvety grass. Evening turned into night. They walked on the wet grass, it was like playing Jesus and walking on the sea.

Lights were on in the house.

Their feet were clumsy. The bed of crushed catmint panted its hot scent. Drops of water trembled on the ferns, a fountain splashed. They crouched and crept. They saw a falling star. They had come all the way from the river.

It was the night of the party. In the supper-room the fluted jellies were jewel colours: amber, ruby.

In the garden they were up to the shaved grass outside the window. A peacock screamed. Their breath pressed against the window and turned it cloudy.

The jewelled jellies gleamed coldly. There were blanc-manges, trifles.

In the garden they remembered how the newspaper

called it an exercise in democracy. As well as Beauville people he'd invited his society friends. Which meant a locket with a diamond star, her diamond-gleaming ears, a diamond so big that when she wore it she had to have a hole cut in her glove. And the newspaper called Valentine Arden a great sentimentalist and it would be a lark, such fun: the party would resemble an out-of-date juvenile one. There'd be a conjurer, a magic lantern, a gipsy to tell fortunes. The servants would be put into the costumes of family retainers of an olden day.

They had walked city squares planning it. Down the long distance of city streets the Hills had mocked them — they were veined with secret gold, but they wouldn't give a pinch of it away.

Cars came up the drive. Doors banged, shoes made a harsh sound on the gravel. The peacocks arranged their tails.

In the garden they hid, they waited. There were diamonds going into the house.

Now there were Beauville people coming. They had come from the little streets — then down the Port Road, past the Chinese gardens. At the gates of Arden House some of them stopped to take off their sandshoes. They hid them in the grass, then put on the best shoes they'd brought with them.

The rich people waited for them, welcoming missionary smiles ready on their polished faces.

In the supper-room there wasn't a hint of anything savoury, not a suggestion of spice. The tall white cake on its tinsel lace doily might have been made of sweet plaster of Paris. The edges of the tablecloth were ruched up in cockle-shell scallops; there were satin bows and baskets of sweetheart roses. Fruit slivers swam in the crystal punch bowl, and were immured in glistening jellies. And there were silver champagne buckets and love cake, snow cake, and small iced cakes decorated with crystallized violets; and cream horns, cream lilies, quivering blancmanges, trifles studded with cherries. Even the bread and butter was sprinkled with hundreds and thousands.

In the black and gold drawing-room people sat on little gold chairs, and Clare couldn't bear to be with them. The grand people smiled at the Beauville people — it was glorious, splendid — but the two sets of people kept apart. Behind the smiles there seemed to be a laughing sense of contempt, a gentle iciness of manner. No one said "I venture to introduce myself" or "Allow me to present". There was a buzz of talk, but at the same time a strange hush and stillness. The Beauville people sat stiff as dolls, but the grand people slouched. They all had the same haughty don't care attitude; there was a wonderful clannish spirit amongst them.

From the beginning, Clare had known it would be horrid. Though Mr Arden's welcome was mannerly, and a young man with powdered hair in a blue velvet coat offered programmes of the entertainment, and a Moorish girl with a necklace of sixpences presented each lady with a posy from her basket. But Mr Arden had his cruel cat look. His eyes were excited, he was planning something — even as he greeted them he looked past them, as if the guest who mattered was yet to come. And in the black and gold room, Mother shrank back. Did she hear the odd little laughs, the well-bred whispers? — "My dear ... her position in the household ... a scandal."

197

Mother was on show, Clare shared her pain. And Aunt Rosa's eyes were tormented because Ralph sat close to Betsy; Uncle Will looked as bad because Peggy and Pompy were there, too, and he mustn't acknowledge their presence. Mr Arden was playing with them all. Aunt Crystal changed colour in a singular manner as an over-dressed puffy lady crossed the room. "Have you seen a ghost?" asked Uncle Jack.

Resplendent in amplitudes of stiff silk folds, Mrs Arden gazed down from the wall; Rudd prowled restlessly, shrivelled and cranky, with her walking-stick and Mr Punch jaw; the caged birds shrilled from the evergreens; "No one could have accepted an invitation to stay in a gentleman's house without loss of reputation ..." Clare couldn't bear to listen; she hid herself away with the sweet things. The grape-vine scalloped sedately round the lacy cake, and who'd believe that those brittle sugary layers enclosed rich fruitiness? Whipped cream, sugar-spun lattices, lily buds ... The garden beyond the window was like a great bunch of black flowers. Swaying, moving. And then she thought she saw faces, and there were little glowing dots — fireflies or cigarette ends? It was imagination, of course, but she ran into the room across the passage.

It was the place Mr Arden liked to retire to. He called it his cosy corner and it was sort of Turkish, with brass gongs, stuffed animal heads, Oriental rugs; an ottoman, velvet cushions, beaded bamboo blinds. The hanging lamps and the incense made it resemble a church, but even there Clare wasn't safe. Someone else was in the dim room, too. Ear-rings and bangles rattled, and she was floaty with veils and scarves, a silver bandage pressed on her painted eyebrows. "You're too early," she said. "It's not time for the fortunes." She came

198

closer, and Clare saw that behind her gipsy disguise she was just the puffy lady who'd upset Aunt Crystal.

The girl was gone, so they came in at the window; one by one they brought their knowing faces into the room. Bubbles of spit came out of their mouths as they crept closer to the table, and it wasn't what they'd come for but they were starved. They dug at jellies with their fingers; they wolfed and gobbled and tilted great slices of sponge at their mouths. The tall white cake towered over them ceremoniously: they were reverent and left it alone. Then they started on the champagne. There was a faraway bee-buzz of voices; a piano rippled and wailed. They'd come to plunder more than a supper-table so they went along passages, they found the stairs. In every room there was something, a hundred things. Solid gold teaspoons went into pockets, a naked lady statuette inside a shirt; they seized Parisian timepieces, an album of flowers from the Holy Land, the silver rose bowl, the Venetian glass fruit bowl. They felt wet and stained with happy fright, their hearts beat giddily, and one squatted to defecate in a neat pyramid. Then they were up to a room with a great bed and they opened doors and pulled out drawers and found Indian silk pyjamas as many-hued as Joseph's coat, a dressing-gown lined with quilted satin ... Garments fluttered in rainbows as they fought over them. Soon they were a picturesque company of knowing ones clad in crimson silk shaving jacket, smoking jacket, poker jacket with silver buttons ... And they found his hats. One wore a billycock with the bow at the back, another a deer-stalker balanced on the tip of his nose, another a highly polished top hat, its

199

curly brim cocked dashingly over an ear ...

The ladies made merry widows in dresses of lace insertion, their skirts swung and swayed and Valentine Arden was the ringmaster, he said Dance, fools, dance. Black Tulip, White Rose, Au Revoir, Californian Poppy — all the scents of the dancers mingled and the Beauville girls dabbed their lipstick with red *crêpe de Chine* hankies.

Dancing, the evening had a joyous atmosphere, but Rosa looked sulky, Dove was so sad, and some of the Beauville men's whiskers looked like seaweed. Then they were modern with the Tile Trot, it was a dance inspired by a cat's moonlight prowl, and Rosa said Disgraceful and fixed them with a basilisk glare. Valentine Arden called Alice his little princess, but he said it sneeringly, and she had to stand up in the silence and recite " 'Twas Roses, Roses". The rich people clapped nicely and said wasn't it wonderful how they could be educated, and there were festoons of laurel leaves, garlands of choice flowers, and the caged birds sang a warning but no one took heed.

Crystal and Alice went off to line up for the fortune teller, while the drawing-room was enveloped in darkness for the magic lantern show. A circle of light wobbled brighter and first the picture was upside down, but then it was "Doggy Drawing Pussy's Likeness", then "Our Puss and her Dog Carriage".

In the cosy corner the fortune teller shuffled the cards and cut, to tell fortunate and unfortunate days.

Then a conjurer, very satanic in appearance, produced cigars from Mr Tostevin's whiskers and an egg from Sticky Thomas's mouth. Wine glasses vanished at his fingertips, goldfish swam in the jug that by rights should have been empty.

And upstairs they were drunk, they were dressed up, they'd been roaming about pinching things. Fortune favoured them and they were blithesome and gay. They lit the candles in the silver candlesticks, and it was like flags of all nations with them dressed in clothes of rainbow hue. Eggy Mitchell anointed himself with butterfly essence; the Joker was a dandy with a little rattan cane. They were exquisites. They were ready for the party downstairs.

In the cosy corner it was dark, Crystal felt hidden. But she was still fluttery, she did not recover herself easily. But of course it hadn't been Hettie ... Girdle of Venus, Ring of Saturn. The fortune teller gripped her hand hard. But the likeness had been a strong one, and brought back the past too vividly. "You went on a journey," the fortune teller said — it was the usual tawdry twaddle. She was cocooned in veils and stayed shadowy. The jewelled lamps glowed; there was a sweet heavy smell. The voice was familiar ... the islands that denoted evil, the little lines relating to children. "I have a lot of things to tell Alice," said Hettie.

And then it was shadow buff, and the large white sheet and the magic lantern were in use again, all the other lights in the drawing-room were extinguished. And they were two parties, now, more than ever, for all Beauville was sent off to be shadows. Dove had to stay in the dark with Valentine Arden and the rich people. They were the images of monsters that fell upon the sheet — but it was only Clare and Rosa and Will Priddle ... but how could she be sure, how could she guess substance from shadow? All about her, people were laugh-

201

ing, but Dove was afraid. The darkness was mazed with a clumsy jostling and pushing. And something glassy shattered, but Valentine Arden only laughed harder (he didn't know it was his Venetian glass fruit bowl that had slipped from Poker Roberts's grasp). The shadows were queerer than ever — they minced foppishly, they waggled their arms, one swung a dandy's cane. And they wore peculiar hats.

Then the shadows all wove together. There was a smell of burning, the room was full of smoke. People were coughing. There was a wild squirmish in the magic square of light and someone was screaming "Fire". The lights went on and people pushed, they fell down, and there was a smoulder, then a blaze, and it had started from a wax candle in a silver candlestick upstairs. Now Valentine Arden's bedroom blazed, the passage blazed. The fire swept down the stairs and there was panic, confusion.

But it was beautiful, with flames flickering in arrows and waterfalls and there were red moons in the flames. Arden House was jewelled with fire, the sunflowers got off the wall — there were sunflowers in the flames, tinsel roses, shaggy chrysanthemums. People were screaming, running backwards and forwards, but they were beautiful as idols — painted gold by the glare of the fire. And there were storms of sparks, sequins; but they had the door open now and the fire chased them into the marbly hall and then the front door swung back to let in the night and all the golden people were mixed up — the Beauville people, the rich people, the river people clung and swayed together as they escaped into the velvety garden. The room blazed like oiled silk. They were little scrambling figures, matchstick people, staggering together. The night blotted them out. They were no longer idols with glittering masks of faces, just little people, shivering, and it was like a page in a book of disasters. Will Priddle clung to Peggy and Rosa searched for Ralph but he was still golden, burning, as he struggled to carry off the great tiered cake. Fiery curtains blew out into the night and Crystal hid her eyes as she stumbled past tangled thickets of flame. Alice had got free; Beryl Doody was ahead of her. And in the sunflowery room Dove opened the doors of gilded cages and birds were fluttering everywhere, the air trembled with their flight. And coming through the smoke was the Joker in his crimson jacket — but it couldn't be true, it was Travice Thorn. Dove held out her hands as he came towards her, and there was the red glare of fire all about them; then they were only tarnished figures, small as ants, under a vast black night sky. And Clare was there, and Mr Tostevin, and there'd been another fire once, another Arden House — it was years ago, but Mr Tostevin still remembered. How the first Arden House burned and Mrs Arden died. But Valentine stayed golden, burnished. He'd climbed on to a chair. He was struggling with the portrait of the old lady and the child. Mama, mama. In the garden Rosa said it was God's wrath. The house seemed to tremble. It was a magic thing, all ruffled. It was a splendid flowering.